THE PULL OF GRAVITY

Gae Polisner

Frances Foster Books
Farrar Straus Giroux
New York

Copyright © 2011 by Gae Polisner
All rights reserved
Distributed in Canada by D&M Publishers, Inc.
Printed in the United States of America
Designed by Alexander Garkusha
First edition, 2011
10   9   8   7   6   5   4   3   2

macteenbooks.com

Library of Congress Cataloging-in-Publication Data
Polisner, Gae.
        The pull of gravity / Gae Polisner. — 1st ed.
            p.   cm.
        Summary: When their friend Scooter dies of a rare disease, teenagers Nick Gardner and Jaycee Amato set out on a secret journey to find the father who abandoned "The Scoot" when he was an infant, and give him a signed first edition of "Of Mice and Men."
        ISBN: 978-0-374-37193-7
        [1. Family problems—Fiction.   2. Death—Fiction.   3. Grief—Fiction. 4. Fathers and sons—Fiction.   5. Steinbeck, John, 1902–1968. Of mice and men.   6. Rochester (N.Y.)—Fiction.]   I. Title.

PZ7.P75294Pu 2011
[Fic]—dc22

                                                                        2010021749

For my boys

Lennie broke in. "But not us! An' why? Because . . .
because I got you to look after me, and you got me to look
after you, and that's why." He laughed delightedly.

—*Of Mice and Men*, John Steinbeck

Go to the center of the gravity's pull, and find
your planet you will.

—*Star Wars*: Episode II, *Attack of the Clones*

1

A fever was what started everything. That, and the water tower, and the cherry cola. Well, also, Dad and his condition, and Mom being in Philadelphia and all.

I mean, the fever alone wasn't the problem, or even the hallucination that came with it. I always got those when I was sick. "Febrile seizures" Mom calls them. But they were usually confined to my bedroom. Okay, once to the bathroom— unless there were actually giant spiders guarding the toilet— and once to the backyard. But there were *definitely* giant noodles dancing out there, so I had to join them. Which, according to my brother, Jeremy, was hilarious.

As far as Jeremy's concerned, I'm just one big ball of feverish entertainment.

Even Mom says she never saw anyone who can spike a fever like I can. It's like I can be fine one minute, then burning up an easy 104 degrees the next.

Jeremy is different. He's Mr. Healthy so it's an international crisis if he even sneezes or gets a headache. Really, the dude is never sick. Never misses a day of school or a game or, worse, his own birthday party. It's like my folks had him, then spent the next three years saving up the sick genes and popped me out to deal with them.

But where was I?

Oh yeah, how everything got started.

So it's the last Friday in August, and I'm a few days from starting high school, which isn't a big deal here in Glenbrook since there's only one elementary school that feeds into one middle school that feeds into Marshall J. Freeman High. So by the time we all get there, we pretty much know everyone by heart. Besides, I'm almost fifteen, so I'm ready to get the heck into high school.

Mom is at Rand Industries where she works, but not at the local factory here in Glenbrook like she normally is. She's at corporate headquarters in Philly where she is the last Thursday through Sunday of every other month, on account of she's their bookkeeper and that's where the bimonthly audit review meetings are held. Well, also, on account of *she has to* since Dad doesn't work much anymore. On account of him being so fat.

Rand Industries is a chemical-by-product storage and removal company, but other than that, there's not much I can tell you about it. Mom's explained it a thousand times, but honestly, I still don't know what they do. Except that a few times a month, a big puff of black smoke comes wafting out of the building, and then a bunch of people run over there with picket signs saying it's bad for the environment. It's not that I disagree with them, but I feel bad for Mom. She doesn't make the stuff. She just keeps the books for them.

Although it is kind of ironic, since clean air and clean living are the main reason she moved us up here to Glenbrook in the first place, right after Jeremy was born.

Anyway, Mom is at Rand headquarters, and Dad is belly-up on the couch in the living room like he always is. Sound asleep, like a beached whale.

I walk over and tap him on the stomach with my lacrosse stick, which I'm carrying around in my boxer shorts because I have this fever and I'm half in—and half out of—sleep, and clearly ramping up to hallucinate.

"Dad, I'm meeting Ryan," I say. "Going out laxxing."

No answer.

I prod him again with the stick. He grumbles and breathes heavy.

"Dad, I'm going out. But maybe I'm sick. Can you feel my head?"

He rolls on his side, his gigantic belly hanging over the edge, and for the millionth time in the last few years I wonder if he's close to dead. But as I head to the front door he manages, "Other way, kid, you'd better go back to bed."

Now if you think I'm exaggerating about the fat part, I'm not. My dad is seriously fat. At last count, 395 pounds of jiggling, miserable fat. And add to that, just plain miserable.

5

Of course, he didn't start out that way. Sure, he was always big, which makes you wonder why I stay so freaking skinny. Barely 110 pounds soaking wet on a good day. Seriously, my ribs show. Not cool for a guy who's entering high school. But Dad was always a jolly sort of big, like a solid 250 or something. Then, after his heart attack a few years ago, he had to take time off because of stress and depression and all, and he got fatter and fatter by the minute. Which was like a vicious cycle, because he lost his job as a desk editor for the Albany *Times Union*, then sat around home writing dinky editorial pieces for the *Glenbrook Weekly Sun*. Which made things worse since the Albany paper was already a huge step down from the New York *Daily News* where he used to work before Mom dragged him up here to "the Sticks." Which is what my dad calls any place more than five minutes away from Manhattan. Where he used to live before Jeremy and I mucked it all up.

But anyway.

So the more I think about it, I guess it wasn't just the fever and the cherry cola and the water tower that got everything started, but also Dad's situation. Or maybe it was actually the Scoot's turn for the worse that really set things in motion.

As hard as I try to pinpoint it, maybe it wasn't one thing that led me to Jaycee Amato and the craziest weekend of my life.

All I know is once it started, it just was.

Spinning in motion, I mean.

And then nothing was the same.

2

So there it is the last week of August, with Mom in Philly, Dad on the couch, and me back in bed, my fever spiking, just waiting to hallucinate noodles. And Jeremy's wherever, which means everything is just like normal.

Even the Scoot is in one of the places he often is, reading in the park on Watson, which is really what saves me in the end. Because I do hallucinate, only this time it's not noodles but a giant can of black cherry cola. Dr. Brown's Black Cherry Soda, if you want to be exact.

I mean, maybe it's stuck in my memory how I used to love that stuff when I was little, how Dad used to bring it home in six-packs every Friday night, and we'd eat pizza and drink black cherry cola until our stomachs were ready to bust. Until Mom banned it, that is, on account of Dad ballooning up big-time.

Only this cherry cola is evil-looking, with long dangling arms and white-gloved Mickey Mouse hands. I know it sounds cute, but it isn't. It's got beady eyes and a black twirly mustache, and it's wielding a machete in its hands.

Which is where the water tower comes into the story. The giant blue, trapezoidal one west of Watson Street that looks like a *Star Wars* AT-AT Walker. Because when Cola Dude starts chasing me, I jump out of bed, fly downstairs and out of the house, down Carver, left on Main, two blocks west on Camelia Street, and right onto Watson, where I run smack into that water tower and start scrambling up to the top.

In my boxer shorts underwear, that is.

Which is bad enough on its own, but these are my Christmas boxers, the red ones with the white polka dots that say "*Ho! Ho! Ho!*" all over them. And it's August. And I'm climbing a water tower in a public park, yelling at a giant invisible cola.

It's not a pretty sight.

But, of course, I'm delirious. I don't know what I'm doing.

I make it maybe twenty feet before someone yells, "Hey, Nick, get down from there!" It's Scooter's high, raspy voice, and somehow it penetrates and I come to. Although not as fully as I need to in order to stop from crashing down.

My leg snaps on impact. Which hurts like a mothertrucker.

But still, I'm pretty lucky. Because the way the Scoot tells it, I'm climbing so fast I'd have reached the top in no time, which is like eighty feet up in the air. And if I'd fallen from there, I'd surely have broken my neck instead of just my leg.

Which is where Dad comes back into the story.

Because he sleeps through it all. Through the fever and the

8

hallucination, and the running, and climbing, and falling, and right through all of Scooter's frantic calls. Even through the ambulance siren racing to get me just a few short blocks away. Through my trip to Mercy Hospital, and the doctors casting me up, and the first of Mom's fuming-angry calls.

You name it, my dad sleeps right through it.

Which leads to Mom coming home early, and to the days and days of screaming. And to Dad packing up and setting out to walk to New York City. And to the news crew showing up, and my collision course with Jaycee Amato.

But first, Scooter saves me, which is pretty ironic because the kid is half-dead himself. Which makes him a temporary hero, instead of a pariah for a change.

So at least some good comes out of it.

Which is nice, because, after that, everything goes downhill.

September 3

Dear Nick,

I've been thinking long and hard the past few months about what I'm about to do. I know I need to do something, anything, other than sit around on the couch waiting for the right answers to come. There's no such thing as a perfect time, so this seems like as good a time and place as any to begin.

I'll be back soon. I hope you understand.

Dad

9

3

But first I should explain the Scoot, so you'll fully understand.

Scooter Reyland is our next-door neighbor and a year older than I am. You wouldn't know it to look at him, though, because he's the smallest, weirdest-looking dude you've ever seen. I'm not being cruel, it isn't a secret. The Scoot would be the first to agree.

The Scoot wasn't born weird, but for as long as I can remember, he's been the messed up way that he is. Jeremy remembers him different, when he was a cute normal baby. But *normal* didn't last very long before total freakishness set in.

By the time I was two and the Scoot was three, he had stopped growing altogether. His head looked too big for his body and his hair fell out, or maybe it never came in. Plus, his skin started to wrinkle and got so thin you could see all the veins underneath. By the time he reached preschool, he looked like a shrunken old man.

And they all watched it happen, Mom, Dad, Jeremy, and worst of all, his mother, MaeLynn. Not me, though. I only remember him the way he is, so he mostly just seems like the Scoot, and not some freakish kid.

Now if you saw MaeLynn, you'd never believe that Scooter was *her* kid. She's a nurse, originally from the South, and looks like a magazine model. Thin, long blond hair, you know the drill. But his mom she was, and the Scoot was her whole entire world.

Anyway, back then, when all this stuff with the Scoot went wrong, his dad, some jerk named Guy, just up and disappeared. Left forever, without even saying goodbye. The way MaeLynn tells it, one day he's there, and the next, he's gone. Period. End of story. He never even calls or sends money.

Dad says he just freaked out, couldn't handle the pressure of what was happening to his son. But MaeLynn says he was lame to begin with, lived in a fantasy world, even before Scooter was born. She says it didn't matter anyway, because his leaving was the best thing for them, that he was a two-bit, wing-flapping chicken who couldn't stand the heat, so better that he clucked on out of her kitchen.

Still, it left MaeLynn to do all the hard work alone. Every week she dragged the Scoot's sorry little ass to doctors, until someone finally told her what was wrong. The Scoot had Hutchinson-Gilford progeria syndrome, which speeds up the aging process and is totally incurable and rare. Like only one in eight million kids ever has it, and the Scoot's got it, so what are his chances there?

It's so rare, MaeLynn says, that in the history of recorded cases, Scooter's is 103rd. I mean, 103 people ever, out of all the *billions* in the world.

Over and over Scooter tries to explain to me how it's caused by this mutant gene that gets copied twice, one time fine, but the other time crazy wrong. I still don't get it. I can't make it stick in my brain.

The other thing Scooter tells me is that he's going to die.

This is years ago. We're like nine and ten, and we're playing Nerf guns in my yard. We're running around and shooting each other, but Scooter has to keep slowing down. Because already the symptoms are bad enough that his heart is weak, so he's constantly short of breath. Suddenly he stops and bends over, hands on knees, all red and panting and wheezing. So I stop too, and he looks up at me and says, "You know, Nick, this mutant gene thing, it's going to kill me soon."

No kidding. Just like that, that's what Scooter says.

Well, of course I don't know it; I don't know anything like it, because I'm just a little kid. Still, I nod my head and say something dumb like "Don't be an idiot, Scooter," then nudge him to keep playing our game.

But I never forget it. I never forget those words.

Anyway, this is how it was. Until a few years ago, the

Scoot was my best friend. Especially on days MaeLynn worked, he was always at our house chilling with me or Dad. Then, near the end of middle school, things changed. We were both really different to begin with, and it was hard enough being a teen. Or, maybe, I finally got a little tired of how he was always hanging around, how Dad seemed to muster more energy for him, and was constantly worrying for MaeLynn. Maybe I resented how it felt like he was somehow our obligation. I started to spend less time with him and more and more time with my other friends.

The Scoot didn't seem too bothered by the shift in our friendship. He still hung around Dad, and Dad welcomed it. Plus, last year, he moved up to the high school, and he was barely in classes by then. Because by fifteen his body is like eighty, and he's older than most kids with progeria live. Seriously, his heart is failing and his liver's shot, which are not your usual teenage problems. So the minute he gets a cough or a cold, or something's just going around, MaeLynn pulls him from school and keeps him home safe with her. And when she's at work, he still knocks around with my dad. Or maybe he heads over to the park on Watson to read or scribble in that marble notebook of his.

Which is what he is doing there the day I break my leg.

Which, of course, leads to the mess with Mom and Dad, and to Jeremy being an ass. And to Dad taking off, and to Jaycee and the six o'clock news.

And to me deciding to do something crazy I wouldn't otherwise normally do.

Or maybe the truth is different.

Maybe I'm itching to do something crazy, and I just need someone to egg me on.

From: FatMan2
To: Nick Gardner
Subject: Walking

Nick,

They say the beginning of any new thing is the hardest. Well,
whoever "They" are, they're right. It is way harder than I thought,
just walking.

More than that, it is hard leaving you guys, hard to be away.

I hope you know that, kid.

But I need to do this. I can't believe I am.

Dad

4

So what happens is Dad morphs into Fat Man 2 and disappears. And just so you know, the whole "Fat Man" thing isn't nearly as original as it sounds.

FatManWalking was actually the user name for this 400-pound guy from California who decided to lose weight by walking across the whole country to New York. For more than a year he walked and lost more than a hundred pounds. At the time, Dad was obsessed with the guy, followed his every move. For months it was all he talked about, like maybe he thought he could do it too.

He didn't, of course, not that any of us believed him in the first place. And eventually, he just stopped talking about it anymore.

Then, a few days after the water tower incident and another screaming match with Mom, he goes and digs out his *Fat Man Walking* T-shirt and starts packing his bags.

"Where'd you get that?" I say. I stand at his bedroom door,

my toes throbbing fat and purple where they poke from my cast, my crutch hiked under my armpit, and watch as he shoves sweats into some high-tech backpack I've never seen before.

He looks up and frowns. "Hey, kid, you startled me."

"Sorry. So, what are you doing? Where'd all the Bear Grylls stuff come from?" I nod at the new hiking things piled up on the bed.

"I'm gonna do it, Nicky. Or at least try. I have to try." He stops packing, sighs. "Now is the time," he says.

"Time for what? When?" My ankle kills. I blink in disbelief.

"I'm aiming for this weekend."

He pauses, then goes back to what he's doing, as if this is all the explanation I need.

A few days later he stands at our front door, his laptop in a new waterproof sleeve, his backpack full, a compact, ultra-lightweight tent bungeed to its frame. I've been up, anxious, all morning, but Jeremy isn't even home. The jerk left for a friend's house without even saying goodbye.

"Figure a month, month and a half tops," he says to Mom. She nods, head down, arms crossed tight to her chest. "Worst case would be end of October. It'll be too cold beyond that." He laughs. "If I make it that long."

"You will," Mom says quietly. She looks up at him now, tightens a strap on the backpack.

Dad nods, looks at me. I shift uncomfortably. He puts his hand on my shoulder which just makes things harder. "Take

17

care of that leg, kid, and don't give your mother any trouble." I nod. After that, he walks out the door.

Mom doesn't seem all that broken up about it. Just goes about her business like usual.

"People have to do what they have to do, Nicholas," she says as we stand at the window and watch him walk down our road. When we can't see him anymore, she ruffles my hair like I'm a little kid and goes back to making us breakfast.

Up in my room, there's a note from him, which I glance at then shove in my desk drawer. And when his e-mails come in, I don't open them at all, just transfer them unread to a file called FatMan2 and act like they never came. I'm not exactly sure why.

Maybe it's because of how much pain I'm in from my leg those first few days, or how Jeremy is constantly being a jerk, but I just can't bring myself to read them. The truth is, I'm pissed at Dad, and not just for leaving me and Jeremy and Mom, but also for ditching the Scoot when he needs Dad the most. Because maybe it sounds like I don't care too much about the Scoot anymore, but I do. Not hanging out and not caring are two very different things.

In fact, with Dad gone, I try to make up for things a little with the Scoot, because who else does he have? Besides, there isn't much else for me to do stuck home in Glenbrook the last few days of summer with a busted leg.

So Scooter and I spend more time together again, mostly talking and watching movies in his living room like we did when we were kids. *Star Wars*, especially, which we can both watch over and over again. Of course, he's in such bad shape the littlest things make him winded now. When he moves and talks, you can hear his insides rattle and wheeze. Neither of us says anything, but it definitely makes me sad.

Luckily, I don't have too much time to think about it, because then school starts up.

The first morning of school is already a bad omen. I wake up way early, like 6:00 a.m. I don't need to be up yet but I can't sleep either, so I get out of bed and gimp downstairs to the kitchen to see if Jeremy's awake. Which he is, drinking coffee and eating breakfast at the table.

I hobble to the cabinet to get myself a bowl and spoon, then hobble over to the table and rest my crutches on the floor, hoping his company will make me feel better.

"Hey," I say, pouring milk in my bowl.

"Dude," he answers.

I don't mind if we don't talk much, really. I haven't slept too well since Dad left, and I'm feeling pretty bummed out and quiet. Maybe it's because I feel responsible for things. Like, if I hadn't broken my leg, then Mom and Dad wouldn't have fought, and now Dad wouldn't be gone. Even though I know this isn't true.

Anyway, the peace and quiet lasts only another minute

19

before my idiot brother starts running his mouth. Says I should stop being so naïve and surprised about Dad going, that anyone paying attention would know he's wanted to leave for years. That he hasn't been happy since Mom made him leave Manhattan, and that Mom hates him anyway, so what's the big deal?

"Kid yourself all you want," he finishes, spooning Cheerios in, "but there's no way in hell he's coming back."

I glare at him, wondering why he doesn't just shut up.

"Yes, he *is*," I finally say, even though I should say nothing, not feed into his annoying bull crap. But he's really pissing me off.

"Nope, Nick, you're wrong. He's gone, trust me. Gonna start a whole new life in New York City. Unless he drops dead first." He shovels in another big, globbing mouthful.

And I snap. I can't help it. When he says this, I just go crazy inside. I pick up my spoon and, without thinking, I chuck it at him. Normally I'd get up and punch him instead, but it would take too long now, because of my bum leg and the crutches. So that's what I do. I chuck my spoon at him.

It hits him hard, smack in the center of his forehead. It sticks for a brief second, then falls and clanks down on the table. A little milk dribbles down his nose.

He jumps up, and I can tell he's about to pummel me— like it's a reflex, you can tell—but then he realizes I'm handicapped, that I've got the broken leg. Plus, now I've got tears in my eyes, so I guess he thinks he should go easy on me. He sits back down and glares. There's a red oval welt where

20

the spoon hit him. I laugh, because it's pretty funny actually, and he glares harder like he's waiting for me to tell him I'm sorry.

"You're an idiot," I say instead, which probably isn't the apology he's hoping for.

After that, neither of us says much of anything. I can't eat now because I don't have a spoon, plus I'm not really hungry. I drag the cereal box across the table anyway, and check the back to see if it has any of those dumb kids' games, like the mazes or the word search or something. I know I'm way too old for that stuff, but I still like to find the hidden objects. Plus, this way, I can ignore Jeremy, which would be a whole lot better. But they're Cheerios, so of course there's nothing but boring health food tips on the back.

Finally I say, "He didn't leave for good, Jeremy. He said he'd be back," because it's either that or sit there and listen to him chew.

"We'll see," he says, but I can tell he's not going to argue.

"There's nothing to see," I say, because I'm not finished yet even if he is, and it's annoying when he acts all superior.

"Whatever, kid. I'm just telling you, so you're prepared. You just don't get how it is." Which bugs me like crazy, because he knows I don't like it when he calls me kid. He raises his eyebrows, but I don't take the bait. Then he says, "Plus there's everything with Reginald, and you know how Dad feels about him. He can't bear to watch that go down."

21

Well, if you haven't figured it out, Reginald is the Scoot, but nobody calls him that anymore. Nobody. Not even Mae-Lynn. He hates it; everyone knows that about him.

"The Scoot," I bark. "You'd better call him the Scoot." I shove my chair out, grab my crutches, and hobble my sorry ass out of there. I mean, you can't pin Dad's leaving on the Scoot. He can't help what's happening to him. Plus, Dad is coming back, so everyone can just move along.

Anyway, that's how breakfast with my idiot brother goes down. Two hours later, I'm in school, and life gets busy, and things pretty much go back to normal.

Until the six o'clock news shows up at our house, that is.

And, with it, Jaycee Amato.

From: FatMan2
To: Nick Gardner
Subject: Walking

Hey Nick,

Yesterday I walked nearly 10 miles, almost to CR-70. Today, 4 more already, so I should be outside of Mechanicville by nightfall.

New York City is roughly another 170 miles by the scenic route.

I'm not sure which is harder, keeping my feet walking, or my mind on the task. I think a lot about you and Jeremy, and the things I'm leaving behind.

The pull of home, and everything familiar, is strong.

Hope the start of school is good, and that your leg is doing better.

Dad

From: FatMan2
To: Nick Gardner
Subject: Walking

Nick,

12 more miles, almost to Troy this evening. I don't know how long I can keep up this pace. It might not seem like a lot, but I have to rest every few hours or my feet swell and my knees start to hurt. Plus, today I have a blister developing on my heel. You'd think you

could walk through a little blister, but it's painful, so I may be sidelined for a day.

Blisters. Pouring rain. The things you forget to plan for . . . Thank God for places with coffee, outlets, and Wi-Fi ;)

Will write again soon. Would love to hear back from you.

Dad

5

The local news wanting to do a feature on Dad isn't as crazy as it sounds.

I mean, before Dad's depression turned him into the Glenbrook version of Jabba the Hutt, he was a well-known news guy around town. He still had connections, and he still wrote some decently big stories every now and then.

In fact, it was Dad who got the Albany *Times Union* to run the series on the Scoot, Dad who wrote it each year, and Dad who kept it all going. Eventually, the series had gotten picked up by the AP and Reuters and ran in some national papers. Even the Sunday *New York Times Magazine* picked it up. I mean, the Scoot was a fascinating kid.

The stories on the Scoot ran every few years, and they were good for the Scoot, but they were also good for my dad. When he worked on them he'd get all enthusiastic in a way I otherwise rarely saw. For days before deadline they'd sit together, Dad interviewing and the Scoot answering into the mic. In the evenings, MaeLynn would come over, still in her white nurse's uniform, carrying piles of updated textbooks she'd brought home from the medical library. She and Dad would sit at our dining room table, drink coffee, and look through them for anything new on Scooter's condition.

Night after night they would work, talking and laughing, until long after the rest of us had gone to bed. Dad seemed so happy at those times, I wondered if Mom noticed it too. Either way, it didn't seem to bother her, I guess, since it was all being done for the Scoot.

Plus, it didn't much matter, because a few days after the story ran, MaeLynn would go back to her double shifts at the hospital, and Dad would go back to the couch, and everyone else would go back to their regular old boring lives.

The point is that there were still a few people who knew Dad around here, so when they heard he had pulled a "Fat Man Walking," it made sense they wanted to cover the story.

At first, it was just the *Glenbrook Weekly Sun* and a paper in Saratoga Springs. But by week two the *Times Union* had picked it up, and then, that following Saturday, News 10 was at our door.

You could tell Mom wasn't too thrilled with the hype, that she was just going along to help Dad. Maybe she thought it would somehow force him to keep walking. The first story read "Another Fat Man Walking: Local Reporter Leaves Family to Save Own Life," which didn't really help the mood around here.

But anyway.

The morning of the interview, I decide to invite Scooter over. I mean, he's sort of family, and it seems like the right thing to do. So there we are, Mom, Jeremy, the Scoot, and me, when the news crew arrives. There are three of them altogether, a cameraman, a producer, and the on-air talent who I recognize as this total tool named J.P. Amato.

Everyone knows Amato. Dad can't stand the guy. He's been News 10's main roving reporter forever. He's about Dad's age, but super fit with a fake tan, a bleached-white smile, and thick blond hair sprayed in place like a big mounded wave of cardboard. He wears a plaid sports jacket, khaki pants, a pink button-down, and brown loafers, like he's going to a yacht club or something, which we don't even have around here. Suffice it to say, he's even more of a tool in person than he looks on the evening news.

But what's more surprising is who walks in with him, which is this girl named Jaycee Amato.

Of course, as soon as I think of her name, I realize who she must be, but the girl looks nothing like her father. I mean, absolutely nothing like him.

Where J.P. is blond and plastic like a Ken doll, Jaycee is dark and quirky. She's pretty—long black hair, cool face— but with a sort of militant edge. Well, that mixed with some

Goth maybe, mixed with some just plain crazy-weird. I've seen her around school a few times but don't know much about her. She's in Scooter's grade, not mine, and no one knows her that well. Rumor has it she showed up halfway through the last school year.

Now, in she walks, camouflage cargo pants, a tie-dyed T-shirt, and bright orange, high-top Converse sneakers, her long black hair in pigtails, and her fingernails painted purple. Plus, she's got this necklace on—if you can call it that—a troll doll tied to string with a hot pink shock of hair.

But what is most noticeable are her eyes. They're this amazing cold gray-blue, like a Siberian husky dog's eyes. They look like glass marbles.

You can't look at Jaycee Amato and not instantly notice her eyes.

"Hey, what are you ogling at?" She jams her hands in her pockets and gives me a look like I've done something wrong. It's bad enough I'm already feeling self-conscious, not only because they're here to do a story on my embarrassingly obese dad, but also because the Scoot is here and he's sort of hard to explain.

I glance behind me to where Scooter sits in Dad's over-sized recliner in the corner, writing in that dumb old note-book of his. He's hunched like a little old man—all three feet three inches of him—the reading lamp shining through his skull. His skin, thin like paper, reveals a road map of purple veins. I wish he'd worn a do-rag like he usually does. He

28

breathes heavy with his mouth open, on account of how everything is failing. He must feel me watching him because he looks up and smiles and flips a casual wave. I force a smile back.

"Hey!" Jaycee says again. I whip my head back toward her, but she walks right past me, and I realize she's talking to the Scoot.

"Hey, Jaycee!" Scooter calls back.

She plops down on the arm of the recliner and pulls the notebook from his hand. And, suddenly, I'm thinking maybe I should rescue him. I mean, who the heck is this girl? But then the producer calls for quiet and tells everyone to take their positions.

They hustle me onto the couch where Mom and Jeremy are, and J.P. moves into the shot. He pats his stiff poof of hair to make sure it's all in place, then clears his throat and begins his lead-in.

The studio lights are bright, and I have to squint to keep my eyes from hurting. I turn my head once more to where Jaycee sits next to the Scoot. She catches me looking and makes a sarcastic face, so I turn quickly back to where J.P. is asking Mom questions. They're pretty tame, like "How is Mr. Gardner doing so far?" and "How many miles has he gone?" Mom gives answers, but they're bland and short, as if she doesn't really want to be here. Which, honestly, neither do I.

After a few minutes the producer yells cut and J.P. wanders away, and the three of them talk in the corner.

I take the chance to shift over and relax, because we're all tense and cramped together like sardines. I feel better with some fresh air circulating. I try not to look back at Jaycee. Instead, I study the stuff Mom's laid out on the coffee table.

There are a bunch of old photographs of Dad and her, and of all of us together. Dad's so much skinnier in a lot of them. One of them is from their wedding, posed in front of a big fancy cake. I pick it up and look at it more closely.

Dad looks nothing like he does now. He's young and smiling, and he actually has a chin. Mom doesn't really look the same either. She's still thin, but in the photo her hair is long and she looks pretty, and her head is way back, laughing. Now her hair is short and pushed behind her ears. She's always so businesslike, a totally different person.

I stare at the photo, wondering how both of them have changed so much, when Scooter walks over and hauls himself onto the couch next to me.

"Hey, Scooter."

He breathes hard, pulls the snapshot from my hand. "Wow," he says, "he's like a whole other guy."

"Yeah, I was just thinking that."

It crosses my mind, sitting here with Scooter, that this is something he completely understands. How someone can be one thing on the inside, while their body morphs and betrays them on the outside. I put my hand on his shoulder and he wheezes.

"Can I see?" Jaycee has come up behind us. She leans over,

her troll thing dangling in my face. My heart races for some reason.

Scooter hands her the photo, and she holds it out in front of her like she's comparing it to the recent photo of Dad they have up on the camera monitor.

"Man, oh man," she says.

I'm about to get defensive, but J.P. is back talking to Mom and calls that we're ready to roll again. They signal for quiet, and Jaycee walks out of the shot, but Scooter stays put with me and nobody seems to mind.

J.P. does a brief re-introduction and starts in with Mom again. "So, Mrs. Gardner, do you think he'll make it to Manhattan, blah, blah, blah," and Mom answers, "Yes, I do, sure, blah, blah, blah," although she doesn't sound too convincing. Then, suddenly, the camera's on me, and J.P. is asking me a question.

"So, Nick, what do you think about your dad's journey?"

I'm caught off guard, so I start stammering. "Oh, yeah, well, sure, it's cool and all that . . ." Then I stop because I can tell I sound like a moron. My eyes dart to Jaycee. She looks down quickly, but not before I see that she's laughing.

I look back at the cameraman helplessly, and he mercifully moves the camera toward Jeremy. "And what about you, son?" J.P. says, sticking the mic in my brother's face.

Jeremy looks down like he's thinking for a second, then looks back at J.P.

"I think you've got way too much gel in your hair, dude," he says, flipping the camera the bird. Then he stands up, squeezes past Mom, and walks out the front door.

I just stare after him, as do Mom and the camera guy and J.P.

But when I glance over at Jaycee again, she's standing there nodding and smiling.

From: FatMan2
To: Nick Gardner
Subject: Walking

79 miles, Nick. Nearly to Hudson! Had to take almost two days
off to let the blister rest, so now I'm stuck trying to make up
time. The scenic routes are longer, but I'm staying off the
highway for obvious reasons. What irony if I got hit by a car.
Now, *that* would be a headline!

Speaking of headlines, I hear my old buds from the *Times Union*
found their way to you guys. Hope that wasn't too painful. And
now the news? Guess I'm a bit of a story.

Mom says school's going okay and you're getting around much
better. Would love to hear back from you, kid.

I miss you,
Dad

6

The Monday after the News 10 fiasco, I run into Jaycee in the Section C stairwell at school. Or, rather, she runs into me. Literally, I mean, which is unfortunate because I'm still in a cast and it's my first day without crutches so I'm feeling unsteady to begin with.

It's like five minutes before the official end-of-third-period bell rings, which makes sense as far as I'm concerned since it's policy to give me a head start on account of my leg. Why Jaycee is roaming the halls early I don't know. But anyway, she is.

She comes barreling down the steps like a lunatic as I'm hobbling up them. Which is how we collide, and I go flying down. Luckily, my backpack strap catches the railing and I fall only a few steps to the landing. I sit there feeling dumb and wait for her to apologize.

"Oh, hey, you're the fat guy's kid," she says.

"Drive much?" I ask, sounding way more lame than I want to.

"Actually, no, but I wish. I'd get the heck out of this hell-hole you guys see fit to call a town." She watches me, thumbs hooked in her pockets, eyes cool and steady. "You remember me, right? I came with the hair gel dude the other day." It's obviously a reference to what my brother said.

"Yeah, I know who you are." I haul myself up. "Sorry about Jeremy. He's an ass. Raised by wolves and all that."

"Doesn't matter to me." She shrugs. "Plus, he's right. The guy is a total doofus."

"Your dad?" I shift my weight. Voices drift down the halls. I'm using up my head start.

"He's so not my dad," she says. Which at least sort of starts to explain things.

"Oh. Well whatever. I'd better get going." I walk past her up the stairs.

"Hey, Nick!" she calls after me.

"Yeah?" I say, a little surprised that she remembered my name.

"Next time, I'll try harder not to kill you."

I see her again that day in the cafeteria, which is weird because I've never really seen her there before. Two weeks into the school year and suddenly the girl is everywhere.

I'm sitting with Ryan and Dan telling them the whole stupid interview story—about how Jaycee showed up and how

Jeremy gave J.P. the finger and walked out, and how the girl is somehow related to Amato—when in she walks and makes a beeline to our table.

I haven't told the guys about the stairwell yet, or anything else about her. To tell the truth, I don't actually know if I'm going to. I mean, Jaycee is a bit of an outcast, and I'm not sure they'd understand. Plus, for some reason, I can't stop thinking about her.

She sits next to me and starts pulling things out of her lunch bag. Like it's normal that she's sitting here; like she does this every day. Dan and Ryan gape at her like gorillas.

"Hey," she says, taking a big bite of apple then talking to me as she chews. "So, I had no idea you were such good friends with the Scoot."

It's not what I'm expecting, of all things, for her to bring up the Scoot. I feel my ears redden. I'm not sure if it's Jaycee's appearance alone that throws me, or the fact that she's barreled in here and tied me to the Scoot. I mean, Dan and Ryan are different from me, and I told you that Scooter could be a mixed bag.

"Well, he's my neighbor," I say.

I don't look at Jaycee after I say it. I already know I'm being a jerk. I'm sure that she can see right through me. I glance at Dan and Ryan instead, but they're too busy shoveling in today's Marshall J. Freeman mystery meat to give a crap about me. I stare at my ham and cheese sandwich instead.

36

"Poor guy," I add so I sound a little more sympathetic. "It's hard to imagine what he's been through."

"I know, right?" She twists a bracelet on her wrist. Her sleeve mostly covers it so it takes me a second to realize that it's not really jewelry, but a Slinky. The classic silver kind. "I think he's awesome. To go through life like that and still be able to do normal stuff, hang out. I really respect the guy. Plus, he's a genius, I'm telling you . . ." She grabs at my sweatshirt sleeve but, thankfully, quickly lets go.

As she talks, I try to figure her out without staring. She's definitely odd. In addition to the Slinky, she has on a troll doll necklace like yesterday, but this one has neon-rainbow-colored hair. Up close, in the bright cafeteria lights, Jaycee's hair is different too, the jet black streaked with bluish purple strands. And she has rings on most of her fingers, but the fake kind with the bright-colored gemstones like you'd get from a gumball machine or the treasure chest in a doctor's office.

I look elsewhere and think of how to change the subject, because I don't really want to talk more about the Scoot. But I can't think of anything, so I pretend to focus on my lunch instead. I take a few bites, but she's holding my sleeve again, and I realize Dan's making a face at me. His eyes go all shifty like he needs to tell me something. I follow his gaze to where Jaycee has a hold of my sleeve with one hand, a Bic pen steadied in the other. She's drawing on me, a small blue skull, not that I gave her permission.

I inspect it. At least it's a decent drawing.

"Anyway, he's seriously dying," she says, pulling my arm back again, "but I take it you already know that." She works at my sleeve some more with her pen, then pushes it back toward me to see. She's added crossbones and a ribbon-type banner that says "R.I.P." inside.

For some reason, it makes me really sad. I mean, there's just been a lot lately, with my leg, and then Dad, and now the Scoot. I run my finger over her drawing, but she yanks it back again, says, "Okay, never mind, hold on."

She leans over it this time, shielding her work from me. I glance helplessly at the guys, but they have looks on their faces that make me want to laugh. Like, *Is this girl crazy, or what?* I shrug and wait till she's finished. Finally, she sits up and pushes my arm back again. The skull has giant ears, a handle-bar mustache, and eyeglasses, so that it looks like a warped Mr. Potato Head. And, where the banner said "R.I.P.," it now says "Get a GR.I.P."

I laugh. I don't know why. I'm completely taken with this girl.

That night, there's an e-mail from Dad like there always is, which I transfer unopened to the FatMan2 folder, then scan through the rest of my e-mails. There are a few dumb forwards from Ryan, some Facebook notifications, and a bunch of junk mail. But I'm stuck on one toward the bottom, which I'm pretty sure is from Jaycee.

I close my bedroom door and open the e-mail.

38

From: JCA
To: Nick Gardner
Subject: Shuffleboard

Hey, Nick. Sorry again about the stairs today. Hope I didn't do
any permanent damage. So, I was wondering if you ever play
shuffleboard, and, if so, can you play with that gimp leg of yours?

Jaycee

From: Nick Gardner
To: JCA
Subject: Re: Shuffleboard

I've played at my grandma's in Florida a few times. Why?

And, btw, what's up with you and all the stuff about the Scoot?

From: JCA
To: Nick Gardner
Subject: Re: Re: Shuffleboard

I know it's crazy, but I have a shuffleboard court in my backyard.
And, yes, I know nobody plays shuffleboard anymore. We also
have a tennis court, a pool, and a trampoline. I mean, a real,
serious, Olympic-grade trampoline. But I'm guessing that's out of
the question with your leg and all?

p.s. That's what you get in return for your doofus of a stepdad
humiliating you every night on the six o'clock news—fancy
backyard toys. And, yes, trust me. It's a *big* price to pay.

From: Nick Gardner
To: JCA
Subject: Re: Re: Re: Shuffleboard

Yeah, I can play. But why are you asking? And what about the Scoot?

And, come on—your dad's not that bad?

From: JCA
To: Nick Gardner
Subject: Re: Re: Re: Re: Shuffleboard

Step dad. And, yes, he is.

Re: The Scoot, I'll tell you Friday. My house, 4:30 p.m. It's the big white one on the southeast corner of Clancy. Tall hedges. Freaking Hummer in the driveway. Trust me. You can't miss it. We're #1. Hah. (That's really the house number.)

From: Nick Gardner
To: JCA
Subject: Re: Re: Re: Re: Re: Shuffleboard

Ok. I'll be there.

    I hit send, then stare at the screen wondering if I just made a date with Jaycee Amato.

From: FatMan2
To: Nick Gardner
Subject: Walking

Nick,

132 miles. It seems impossible, but it's true. My sneakers prove it.
Already on my second pair and you can see the wear on those . . .

Some days I walk 3–4 hours straight. Then rest and walk some
more. I've done some reading, and jotted ideas for articles. Thank
God for Internet cafes and my iPhone and Juice Pack.

I get it if you're mad at me, Nick, but I needed to do this. I could
really use your support. I've done a lot of thinking and we all have
lots to talk about when I get home. But first, to finish this.

I miss you and love you,
Dad

From: FatMan2
To: Nick Gardner
Subject: Walking

Nick,

160 miles. 2½ pairs of sneakers.

At least 10 e-mails from Scooter and even a text or two from
Jeremy. And not a word from my other son. I expect this crap
from your brother, but you?

Dad

7

As instructed, that Friday I show up at Jaycee's house promptly at 4:30 p.m.

Jeremy drives me. With Dad gone, he gets free use of Dad's car, but as part of the deal he has to take me where I need to go. Especially now, while I can't bike or walk that far. Although the good news is, my leg is way better. Still casted and all, but at least I can get around.

Jeremy's pretty good-natured about the chore. He actually says a few words to me as we drive, which is more than he usually does, but neither of us mentions Dad. We've been pretty careful not to do that since I chucked the spoon at him. Finally, I point out the huge white house on the corner of Clancy Street.

"Holy crap! Look at this place," he says. "I think you may have scored, kid." I laugh even though he calls me kid. I mean, big deal that he's a senior and next year he's out of here to some college in either Boston or Manhattan. I get out of the car and tell him that I'll text him when I'm done.

As for the house, Jeremy's right. The thing is enormous. The girl was not exaggerating. I gimp up the sprawling lawn and brick steps to the front entrance, which is framed by two huge stone columns. It feels like I'm about to walk into a museum.

I reach for the bell, but the door opens. Jaycee stands there smiling. "Gardner," she says, "very punctual. Come on in, nobody's here, but my mom will be home soon."

Inside, it's not what I'm expecting. Right behind Jaycee there's a gigantic, gold-framed mirror above a small fountain, with actual running water. In the middle of the fountain, there's a green statue of a cherub. Like Cupid, only this one's holding a fish. Water spouts out of its mouth. And above us hangs an enormous chandelier.

"Cool," I say, looking from one to the other.

"Completely hideous," Jaycee says, pulling me to lead me up the stairs. Halfway up, she stops and looks back at me. "Hey, can you make it up all of these?"

"Yeah, I can," I say, nudging her.

As I follow her, I wonder what on earth I'm doing inside Jaycee Amato's house. I mean, a few days ago I didn't even know her. Not that I do now.

I watch her as she climbs the stairs. She's dressed pretty normal for Jaycee. A green Marshall J. Freeman hoodie, jeans, her orange high-tops and her black hair in pigtails. Except I noticed at the door that she's replaced her troll doll necklace with a Hello Kitty figurine, one of those little plastic white cats with a red bow on its head that looks like a Japanese cartoon? It's tied to black string and hangs crooked by its neck like it's committed suicide or something.

At the top of the stairs, we turn left and pass a fancy bathroom and a master bedroom—both spotless and huge—before we reach Jaycee's room. I don't think I've been inside a girl's bedroom, at least not since I was little. It surprises me how pink it is. Girly, fairy-princessy pink. Which seems nothing like Jaycee.

"No comment," she says, reading my thoughts. "I didn't pick the color."

"No?"

"Are you nuts?" She plops on the bed, which is made up with a frilly pink and lavender checkerboard bedspread, but I stay put in the doorway. "This whole atrocity belongs to the Doofus," she says, motioning around. "My mom and I just moved in last year. And this was the Kook's room. Before she went to college."

"Oh," I say, trying to keep it all straight, "the Kook?"

"His daughter. An-ge-li-ka." She breaks up the name into separate syllables and makes a crazy sign at her ear. I decide this isn't the best subject to keep asking about.

"At least he's rich," I try.

"Big deal. We already had money. And where did it get me? Stuck in this place with these wackos, that's where." She picks up a small pink pillow and holds it out toward me. It's embroidered with a black crown covered in colorful rhinestones and says DADDY'S PRINCESS on the front. She rolls her eyes and tosses it on the floor.

"Can't you paint it?" I know it's not really her point, but I'm not sure what else to say.

"Can't be bothered. Besides, I keep hoping we're not staying."

"Really?"

"I don't know," she says.

"Where were you before?"

"New York City. I love it there. And I hate it here."

I think about Dad suddenly, and what Jeremy had said about how Dad hasn't been happy since he left Manhattan. It makes me want to argue with her about how the city's not so great. But I don't, because I don't want her to think I'm some sheltered kid who doesn't know what it's like there, since I do. Even though I've only been there a few times. I've seen enough to know I don't get the big deal. I mean, what's so bad about Glenbrook?

"Come on. Never mind about that," she says, as if she knows what I'm thinking. "Don't stand there. Come in, sit down." She pats the bed. I feel weird, but I sit next to her. Thankfully, she pops up again. "Here, you stay, I'll show you what I called you here for, then we'll go play some shuffle-board."

Jaycee walks to her closet and slides out a step stool. She pulls something down from the top shelf and jumps back to the floor.

"Here," she says, walking over, but I can already tell what she has. I recognize it immediately, or at least I think I do. It's a black and white marble notebook. *Scooter's notebook.*

"What the heck?" I say.

Jaycee hands it to me. "Go ahead, open it." I look at her suspiciously, as if she's telling me to do something illegal.

"Why do you have this, Jaycee?"

"He gave it to me. I promise. It's easier if you read first. I'll explain more after. Just let me do this my way." She pulls the book from me, opens to the first page, and places it on the bed in front of me.

The top of the page has a date from like two years ago. I read.

Dear Dad,
*   No matter what anyone says, I don't think*
you're a bad person.

I stop reading and glance up at Jaycee, confused.

"He never sent it," she says. "It's just a draft. Keep going."

She nods at it, but it's uncomfortable reading Scooter's private words, especially these. It feels wrong. Then again, she has the notebook, and she says Scooter gave it to her, so it must be at least sort of okay.

"Then stop watching me. It's weird."

She rolls her eyes but walks away, plops herself down on the floor against her closet door. I force my eyes back to his notebook.

> *I get it, why you left, I truly do. Who can sit around and watch this happen to their kid? See him get teased and ostracized, then get sick and die? I'm sure that's too much for most mortal people.*

I look over at Jaycee again, I can't help it. She smiles in this sweet, sad way, so I keep going.

> *But that's not my truth. Actually, my life is pretty normal and happy and good. I go to school. I write. I read. I have a great mom and a few good friends. So, I really don't suffer too much. And I don't want you to lose me for good thinking that my life was only sad.*

My throat gets a lump in it and tears well in my eyes. I don't look at Jaycee anymore. I just want to finish the page.

> *And as for dying, well, I guess I just don't get why everybody is so freaked out by it. We're all going to die sooner or later. I'll just do it sooner. As*

someone wise once said, "Death is a natural part of
life."

I laugh, because I know he's quoting Yoda like he always
does. *Revenge of the Sith*, Episode III.
"What?" Jaycee asks.
"Nothing."

So, anyway, I hope I can find you and get to
know you a little while I still have some decent
time left. I'm guessing I don't have too much.

I feel Jaycee's eyes on me, checking for my reaction, or
maybe to see if I'm done. I skim down. There's only a little
left to read.

If I don't find you in time, I'll leave this letter for
you, and the book, which I really wanted to give
back. Maybe one day you'll get them and know me
for who I am.

With love from your son,
Reginald "the Scoot" Reyland

I push the notebook away and look up at Jaycee. "Jeez," I
say. It's pretty much all I can manage.
"I know, right?" She walks over and scoops the notebook
from the bed.

49

"But what's the point? He wants him to have the note-book? Besides, why do you have it, anyway, and why are you showing it to me?"

"Patience," she says, "hold on." She flips to another page and hands it back to me. "First this." She points. "And no, not the whole notebook, just the letter. Trust me, there's more."

I obey, and focus again on Scooter's tight print:

Information as to Dad's Whereabouts:
- *Google search, Guy Reyland. Results 0.*
- *Google search, Reyland + Rochester, one listing. W. Reyland. No info.*
- *Google search, White Pages, A. Reyland, Rochester. 414-555-0707. No answer. Repeated tries.*
- *Number disconnected.*
- *(!) Rochester White Pages (thank you Glenbrook Library). Reyland, A. 3625 First Street. 414-555-0707. Number still disconnected.*

"So what?" I say when I'm finished.

Jaycee snatches the notebook again and carries it back to her closet. She feels around for something else, jumps back down, and walks over to the bed and sits down next to me, putting a small velvet pouch in my lap. She smells like straw-berry. I hadn't noticed it before.

"Go ahead," she says, "open it."

The pouch is purple with a gold braided closure and clearly holds a book. I sigh and undo it. At this point, I know better than to ask another question.

Inside is a musty hardcover book. Pale blue with an old-fashioned drawing of two men in hats, one big, the other small, walking down an orange road. In the background are some roughly sketched mountains. In bold black letters it reads *Of Mice and Men, a Novel by John Steinbeck.* It's obviously one of those dumb classics the Scoot is always reading.

"Okay," I say, turning it over, "*now*, so what?"

Jaycee takes it from me, studies it for a second like she's thinking, then puts it back in its pouch and underneath her pillow.

"Never mind," she says. "Let's play some shuffleboard before it gets dark. I'll kick your ass while I'm telling you."

The backyard is huge. Like ten of ours. To the right is a tennis court, and next to that, as promised, an enormous trampoline. Not like the normal little round ones lots of people have. This is the huge, rectangular kind they use in gymnasiums. The netting must be fifteen feet high. I stop to stare, but Jaycee tugs my arm and drags me in the other direction. We pass a covered Olympic-size pool. I whistle and she says, "See, I told you."

Beyond that is a garden area, mostly dying plants and

shrubs now, with a pond and another running waterfall. And then, farther downhill, the shuffleboard court and the structure that Jaycee refers to as the shed. Which is hilarious because the thing is more like a small house, with windows and a fancy white-paneled door.

"Unbelievable," I say.

"Insane."

My mind spins. I mean, my dad was a newsman too, and we never had half of this stuff. And worse, J.P. isn't even a real newsman, just the on-air talent. A no-brains talking head, as Dad would call him. Figures he gets paid so much more.

When we reach the shed, Jaycee says, "You'd better wait out here. It's dangerous in there." She ducks in, laughing, then bangs around and emerges with two long gold shuffleboard poles and a rack of red and blue disks. "Here, you take the cues. You can use them as crutches," she says.

We walk to the courts, and I sit on a bench on the sidelines. "Okay, Gardner, blue or red?" She clangs the disk carrier down next to me.

"Blue." I gather my four and head to the far side of the court.

I beat her two games to one without a single word about the Scoot being mentioned, before I demand we stop and sit again so she can fill me in. Besides, it's starting to get dark. As if on cue, the lights surrounding the court switch on.

"Did you do that?" I ask.

She shakes her head. "Sensors. Timers. Thousands of dollars of essential recreational electricity."

"Right," I laugh.

"So, you didn't tell me you were a ringer." She sits next to me, so close that her knee touches mine. I can't stop looking at it there. I shove my hands in my pockets, and she pulls her hood up and her sleeves down over her fingers and shivers. It's officially fall. You can feel the sudden chill in the air.

Up close like this in the bright, artificial lights, I can see Jaycee's eyes and something I hadn't noticed before. Her right eye has a pale gold ring around it, between the pupil and the ice blue iris, so that her eyes appear two different colors.

"Weird, I know," she says, winking the left eye shut, then the right one. "They're totally different depending on the light." I turn bright red. I didn't know I was staring.

"They're cool. I just never saw ones like that before."

"They're from my dad. My real dad. Not Mr. Perfect up there." She motions toward the house and sighs.

"You really don't like him," I say. She shakes her head. "So how come you use his name?"

She shrugs. "It makes my mom happy. And there are perks. So, what's the difference? Using my real name isn't gonna bring my dad back." She pulls her arms into her sleeves so that the empty ends hang over her hands, then wraps them tightly around her chest.

"What happened to your real dad?"

"Motorcycle." She pauses, looks past me at the sky. "Or truck, I guess. I mean, it was more the truck than the motorcycle." She laughs, but it's not the funny kind of laugh, more the kind you force yourself to do because it's either that or cry. "I barely remember him. I was only five."

"That sucks," I say, because I'm not sure what else there is. Then we both sit quietly for a minute, until Jaycee perks up again.

"Hey, so here's a riddle for you." She slaps my shoulder with the limp end of her sleeve. "What do Jaycee Amato, Nick Gardner, and Reginald Reyland all have in common?"

And then I get mad. Because if she really knew him, she'd know not to call him by his real name.

"The Scoot," I say. "He hates it when people call him Reginald."

"Sorry." She nudges my leg with her knee. "I was just joking. So, what's the answer? Give up?"

"Yeah, I give up," I say.

"Now, none of them have their fathers around."

"My father's around!" I snap back defensively. I don't think about it, just blurt it out, then feel bad because why don't I just rub it in? But I'm getting kind of frustrated too. I mean, she shows me all this weird, important stuff, and now she's just horsing around. I don't even know why I'm here. I stand up and start gathering disks into the carrier.

She grabs my arm. "I know, Nick," she says softly. "I was just kidding. I know with your dad it's only a temporary thing. I was trying to make a point, that's all."

"Which is?"

"That it sucks not to have your dad around. Sucks for me, sucks for you, and sucks completely for the Scoot."

"And?"

"And, that's why I asked you to come."

"Because . . . ?"

"Come on," she says, grabbing up the rest of the stuff. "Let's put this away and go back in. I'll tell you the rest up there."

I follow her back through the yard, trying to be patient. What choice do I have? It's clear she's going to do things her way. As we walk toward the house, I pull out my cell phone and check the time. It's nearly six o'clock. This section of yard is dark. The Doofus's electricians didn't wire this part for sound. My stomach rumbles.

"I'd better call home," I say.

"Give me a half hour before you go."

It rings four times and I get the machine, leave Mom a message telling her I'm at Ryan's and that we're working on a science lab. Then I text Jeremy's cell.

"How come you lied?" Jaycee asks when I hang up. "Won't Jeremy tell her where you are?"

"It was just the machine. Didn't feel like explaining. And my brother, you mean?"

"Yeah. He drove you here, right?"

"Yeah," I say, "but I'm lucky if he'd tell her if I died."

"Really?" She sounds surprised.

"You don't have older siblings, do you?" I say.

She laughs. "Well, in that case, it might just help us with our plan."

"Great," I say. "If only I knew what that was."

From: FatMan2
To: Nick Gardner
Subject: Walking

Nick,

168 miles. Another blister, another waylaid day. But still, barely thirty miles from the tip of Manhattan.

My sweats are too big. I had to stop and buy new ones. A very good sign.

Honestly, I'm tired. And pretty much every part of me hurts. Maybe I'm pushing too hard.

Taking the day off today, holed up in a Days Inn. I just needed a real bed for a change. Only my third since I left.

I've spoken to Mom and MaeLynn. I hear Scooter isn't doing too well. And that you've been a good friend. The kid is tough. I admire him.

Also hear your leg is healing nicely. I'll bet you'll be happy to get that cast off soon.

Miss you.

Dad

8

The smell of good food hits me as soon as Jaycee opens the back door. We walk toward the kitchen where a woman I assume is Jaycee's mom is cooking something at the stove. Sautéed garlic, onions, and meat sauce fill my nose. My stomach grumbles loudly.

"Hi, Mom!" Jaycee calls. The woman whips her head around.

"Oh, hey, sweetie," she says.

She's not what I expected, not that I gave it much thought. I mean, she's pretty, but except for that and her long, dark hair, she doesn't look much like Jaycee. Maybe because she's so preppy-looking. She's in tennis clothes—a short white skirt and white polo shirt with pearls around her neck and a ponytail, like she totally belongs at a country club. Which makes sense, I guess, given the Doofus and all. Except for her feet, that is. Because when she walks to the fridge, I see she's got on these giant blue, fuzzy bedroom slippers. So at least I see where Jaycee gets that from.

"You must be Nick," she says. "I'm making spaghetti and meatballs. I hope you'll stay?"

Jaycee gives me bug eyes which I take as a sign to decline.

"Thanks," I say, "but I probably have to get home."

Jaycee uses my science lab excuse, and we head back up to her room where she closes the door behind us.

"Won't your mom mind?" I glance nervously at the closed door. She shakes her head.

"Go ahead, sit. We've only got a few minutes." She points to the bed again. My leg throbs from all the walking and standing, so I'm happy enough to give in.

"So," she says, backing up and leaning against the Kook's pink wall, "the plan is, you and me, Nick, we're gonna find Scooter's dad."

I hear her, but I don't. Or at least I hope I don't, because what I think I hear is crazy. And yet the minute she says it, I know something else. That whatever she wants, she's going to make it happen, and it doesn't matter what I have to say or how I argue, because I'm already at her mercy. My gut knows this, but my brain doesn't want to believe.

"Seriously, you're cuckoo for Cocoa Puffs," I say.

"Excuse me?"

"Cocoa Puffs. You're cuckoo for Cocoa Puffs, Jaycee."

"Like the cereal?" She rolls her eyes.

It's dumb. I don't know why I say it. It's what Jeremy always says to me. I pull up the bottom of my jeans and slide my fingers into the top of my cast to try to reach an itch, but I'm really stalling for time. I feel her staring and waiting.

"Okay, why?" I finally manage.

"Because he wants us to. And he's dying. Isn't that enough?" I roll my eyes at her melodrama.

"How do you know?"

"Because he told me. And he gave me his stuff." She reaches under her pillow and pulls out the purple pouch.

"Right," I say, "and what does the magic book have to do with everything again?"

I know I sound like a jerk, but a few days ago, I didn't even know this girl and her crazy-fountained house, and I still don't get the connection between her and the Scoot. Until the news crew showed up, I didn't even know that she knew him so well. Or that Scooter knew her. Now, suddenly, she's his best friend—make that his fairy godmother—trying to grant him some ridiculous dying wish! And, worse, trying to drag *me* in.

"He wants us to give it to him. To his dad. Guy Reyland. He's been trying to find him for years. I mean, he's looked for him, not that hard I guess, but Googled him and stuff. But not much luck, as you saw. And now he needs us to do this for him. He wants us to."

"Us?"

"Okay, me. But he talks about you. He hinted that you might help me."

"Great," I say.

"He's dying, Nick."

"I know that, Jaycee." My voice cracks. "I know the guy a lot longer than you. I know he's dying."

"I know you do," she says, "at least when you're not in denial."

"A river in Egypt," I say.

"What?"

"Never mind."

I get that I'm being annoying, but I can't get my thoughts straight. Jaycee's got me upset, and I don't even know why. I need more information.

"Okay," I say, "then why doesn't he just ask MaeLynn?"

"He has. Well, sort of. Here and there. She tells him she doesn't know. And doesn't want to know. And he doesn't want to push her and make her more upset. It's not really a happy subject for her. He's already worried about her. You know, how she'll be when he's gone."

I swallow. I don't want to talk about that. "Okay, why you, then? Why did he ask *you*?"

She stares hard at me. "Because he couldn't ask you," she says.

"What does that mean?"

She gives me a wiseass look, but smiles too. "It means you're you," she says.

"Jeez, what is *that* supposed to mean?"

She twists her Hello Kitty necklace then chews on its head thoughtfully for a second. "Nothing really, I guess. Mostly, it means you're a guy. That's all. I mean, here you are, you've known the kid his whole life. And I've known him a few months. Yet, somehow, I know him better than you. You gotta admit it's the tiniest bit pathetic."

"Be careful," I say, nodding toward her necklace, "I bet that's made in China and you're sucking on deadly levels of lead."

She inspects it, then drops it. "You're probably right," she says.

"So then I'm not a total asshole."

She laughs and sits down on her bed and faces me. I smell the strawberries again.

"I didn't say that, Nick. Come on. I just feel bad for the Scoot, that's all. He's my friend. And he's been your friend even longer. I just want to help him." She looks away for a second then turns back. Her gray-blue eyes have filled with tears. "And I don't think he has too much time."

"Fine," I say. "What do you need from me?"

"Your help. I don't think I can do it alone."

I sigh, because it's clear there's no turning back from here.

"So then, how exactly does the book come in?"

"Oh yeah," she says. She swipes at a tear and pulls the

book from its pouch and studies it like she needs to be reminded. "If we find him but he won't come back with us, he wants us to give it to his dad."

She places the book in my lap. I stare at its bland blue cover with the illustration of the men. It looks boring. Why does Scooter care if we get some dumb old book to his dad? My stomach growls again, embarrassingly loud. I glance at my cell. 6:30 p.m. I text Jeremy, remind him to pick me up in ten.

"It's a first edition," Jaycee says while I finish typing. She flips it open in my lap to the title page and points. "Signed by the author, see?" Under her finger, in large black script, is his name, *John Steinbeck.*

"Cool," I say, "but so what?"

"It's worth a ton of money, Nick."

"Really?"

"Like fifteen thousand dollars, really," she says.

"Fifteen hundred, you mean."

"No, Nick. You heard me. Fifteen thousand. At least."

"You're kidding. Are you sure?"

"Pretty sure. Scoot and I Googled it. We found three others like it. Two were worth around twelve thousand and one was worth fifteen. Because they have the original dust jacket and some important typo on page 9 they call the 'pendula.' But those were in good condition, and this one is in perfectly mint condition. So, this one could be worth even more."

"Wow," I say. I don't have a clue what she means, but she sounds like she does. I close the book and study the cover again. There they are, the two men in hats, one big, one small, walking down the boring orange road.

"But if it's so valuable, why doesn't he leave it with Mae-Lynn? Because, no offense, but his dad is a lowlife nobody. His dad ditched him, Jaycee. He should keep it and give it to MaeLynn."

I'm riled up, suddenly. I mean, MaeLynn worships the kid. His dad never did a thing for him his whole entire life.

"Except give him the book," Jaycee says, even though I know I haven't spoken that last part aloud. I look at her, surprised. "Yeah, I know. I was surprised too. But it's true. The book was from his dad. Apparently Guy Reyland loved literature, go figure. He found that edition before Scooter was born. Left it for him when he took off. Maybe so he'd have something worth anything."

"Really? I don't picture the dude even reading. More like some drunken dumbass."

"Convenient," she says, "but it's not always that simple." I give her a look, but as always she gives it right back. "You want it to be that simple, Nick. Right or wrong. Good or bad. But sometimes it just isn't. Maybe it's possible that his dad was messed up, but that he was also a smart, decent guy."

"Who ditched his kid. His dying, freak-of-a-mess kid. And never checked back in."

"Well, your dad just ditched you."

"It's temporary," I shoot back. "And *I'm* normal. I'm not like the Scoot." The minute I say it, I know how it sounds.

"Scooter's normal," she says.

"Give me a break, Jaycee, you know what I mean." She rolls her eyes, pulls the book from my hands, puts it in its pouch, and returns it to her closet. When she's done, she stays there, arms crossed, waiting.

"Look, yes or no? Are you going to help me or not?"

"To find a guy we never met, and have no idea where he is, or really where he might be? Carrying a fifteen-thousand-dollar book with us? Sure, why wouldn't I, Jaycee? It's a great idea. Have you even discussed this with the Scoot?"

"Well, sort of, but not exactly. He gave me the book for safekeeping. Said he's still looking for his dad, but knows he has to face the fact that he's not likely going to find him. And, that if he doesn't, if his dad ever shows up here, then I should give this stuff to him. The book and a copy of his letter." She sounds like she's going to cry. "He may not have directly asked me to do it, Nick, but he's secretly hoping I will. I know it. He needs this now. He needs me to do it. And I need you. I don't want to do it alone."

I take a deep breath. I still can't believe we're having this crazy conversation. I mean, how are we supposed to just go off and scour the globe for Scooter's dad? I stand up to leave before I agree to something stupid.

"Scooter's pretty sure he's in Rochester," she blurts. "It's not that far."

I stop at the bedroom door. "Jeremy's probably here. I'd better get going."

"So?" Her cool blue eyes stare into me.

"I gotta go," I say.

She follows me downstairs, unlocks the front door, and walks out into the fresh air. Jeremy is just pulling around the corner in Dad's blue car.

"Nick, yes or no? Are you in?"

I shake my head at how crazy it all is, but even as I do, I know.

"Jaycee, why are you even asking? Do I really have a choice?"

"No." She smiles. "No choice at all."

"Well then," I call, heading down the walkway to my brother, "I guess that means I'm in."

From: FatMan2
To: Nick Gardner
Subject: Walking

Nick,

196 miles! New York City here I am!

Took me a little longer than expected. Sprained my ankle tripping
over a pebble (I swear, it was no bigger than my thumb). Took me
three-plus days to get back on the road. But I'm here. I made it.
That's all that matters.

It's so good to be back in New York City. The place is humming and
alive, just like it always was. You should have seen me, Nick,
blubbering like a big old baby when I reached the West Side
Highway.

I'm exhausted, but feel better than I have in years. Going to treat
myself to a few days here, I've decided. Say hi to a few old
colleagues. My friend Jack Miller from the *Daily News*—don't
know if you ever met him?—said I can stay downtown with him.
Once I get settled, I'll call you all and say hello. But too early now.
As you can see from the note it's barely 5:00 a.m. And I haven't
slept much these past few days.

Could use a shower bad, so once the hour is decent, I'll head
down to Jack's apartment. In the meantime, just having a cup of
Joe and taking in the sights and sounds of NYC.

New York City, Nick! The Big Apple never looked so good. I
walked here, start to finish. I don't know how.

I miss you and love you,
Dad

9

Now that I've agreed to help with her crazy plan, Jaycee and I meet almost daily, except for the days that one of us hangs out with the Scoot. We try to keep things the same as much as possible. She doesn't tell him about us or our plan and, of course, neither do I. She doesn't want him to try to talk us out of it, or worse, to get his hopes up too high, since so far we've found nothing further on his dad.

Although Guy Reyland continues to be a mystery, at least I find out how Jaycee and Scooter got to be such good friends.

"Oh, that? Art club," she says. She leans over me as we search on her computer, her Slinky Special Anniversary Edition bracelet jangling in my ear. "Hey, try this one." She points to something on the screen, as if we haven't already tried it or something like it nine thousand times before. We've plugged the name Reyland into every major search engine we can think of, not to mention Twitter, Facebook, and Myspace. We're mostly interested in any Reylands we can find in Rochester, since he apparently grew up there, and that's where Scooter thinks he'd be. We've come up with a ton of weird stuff, including some family tree with names dating back to the 1800s but no Guy, and some official business-looking thing with the Secretary of State in Albany. It gives a block and lot number on Front Street in Rochester, but once we search further, the only name that appears in connection with that is some corporation. And, of course, we find the A. Reyland on First Street that Scooter had written in his notebook, but we get a recording that the number is changed and the new one is unlisted. Still, I obey Jaycee and click on the link she points to. It turns up nothing helpful.

"You do know Scooter was in art club, right?" She sighs and flops onto the Kook's checkerboard bedspread. "Mondays after school, with Mrs. Martinez? The dude can really draw."

I know what she's talking about, the after-school club. But I had no idea Scooter was in it.

"Scooter stays after? He's barely in school these days."

"Well, not this year. He only made it to the first one."

"So, you hung out there?"

"There and here," she says.

"Wait, Scooter's been here?"

"Yeah. All summer. What's with the shock, Gardner? He's not too bad at shuffleboard."

"You're kidding me." I turn to her.

"No. Why?"

"No reason. He just never mentioned it."

She sits up, rolls her eyes. "Well, I'm sure you didn't ask."

As for the Scoot, he's not doing so good. He's caught a cold again, a nasty one he can't seem to shake. It's moved into his chest; you can hear it rattle around in there. The guy is suffering. You can tell it's wearing him down. And as much as I know what's coming—knew forever ago to prepare—it kills me to watch it happen.

Scooter's good-natured about it though. I mean, that's one thing you gotta know about the Scoot. He doesn't complain. And he doesn't want anyone to feel sorry for him. And he doesn't feel sorry for himself.

In the meantime, Dad calls to tell us he's made it to New York City. He speaks to Mom, but I'm not in the mood. I'm happy for him and all that, but something about it makes me sad in the pit of my stomach. When we finish what we need to do for the Scoot, maybe I'll deal with it then.

Knowing that Jaycee isn't around on Mondays after school, I make it a point to spend those afternoons with the Scoot. We mostly watch movies at his house. Of course, Scooter is still on a *Star Wars* kick, even more than he used to be. Both of us were crazy for it when we were little, but he never really grew out of his obsession. We watch them back-to-back, over and over again. He mouths the words, has all the lines memorized, especially anything Yoda says. I don't complain, even if I'm slightly sick of them.

"You know, I finally get it, Scoot," I say during one of our marathons. "Your *Star Wars* obsession, I mean. You look exactly like Yoda." I punch his arm softly to let him know that I'm joking.

He turns to me all serious, like maybe I actually hurt his feelings, but then squints and smiles and bows his head. "When nine hundred years *you* reach, Nick Gardner, look as good, you will not." Even on his deathbed he has me laughing.

As the second week of October arrives, Jaycee and I start to map out the actual logistics of our plan. Even though we have nothing concrete on Guy Reyland, we keep moving forward with ideas. It's clear that Jaycee won't be deterred.

"We need to go there, Nick," she says. "And we need to go soon. I'm not kidding. It's not a big city. If we ask around we'll find someone who knows him. Or knows someone who knows him."

"Yeah, only 200,000 people," I say. "That should be easy to narrow down in an hour or two."

"Well, we'll have a couple of days."

I don't try to argue with her anymore. I mean, Jaycee's convinced that Guy Reyland is in Rochester and we're going to get there and find him, and that, when we do, he's going to give a rat's ass and follow us back to Glenbrook to say one last goodbye to his son. So, at this point, there's nothing to do but hope for the best and go with it.

Jaycee decides we should leave in two weeks, the last Thursday of October. My cast comes off before then, so my leg will be ready.

"Plus, that way, your mom will be in Philly," Jaycee says. "So if we need it, we'll have Thursday *and* Friday, too. That gives us four whole days to find him."

"Or to not find him," I remind her. I can't help myself. Somebody's gotta keep *her* hopes in check. She just gives me a look and continues.

"We can always come up with an excuse for the weekend. That should be easy. You'll say you're at Ryan's, and I'll say I'm anywhere. I'll make up a girlfriend from school. My mom will be so pleased I've made one, she won't even care who it is. I'll check in periodically by cell."

"That works for you, but what about Jeremy? We have school Friday. He'll be watching me, you know."

"I thought you said he wouldn't even notice if you're dead?"

"Good point," I say.

Jaycee informs me there's a Trailways bus weekdays from Albany to Rochester that leaves at 6:30 a.m. So all we need to do is get to Albany, which is about an hour away. Jaycee says she'll pay for a taxi. We'll have to leave around the same time Mom leaves for Philly, so if she asks why I'm up, I'll tell her I'm going to extra help before school. I'll spend the next two weeks building up the story, so I don't really think she'll question me, or care. She's so crazed on those days trying to get everything prepped for the long work weekend. As long as I tie it to school, it should be okay.

As for the bus fare and other expenses, I've got a few bucks saved, but not really enough to help much. Jaycee says not to worry. She says she's got a whole bunch of birthday money saved up, not to mention her own debit card, and that she'll cover everything, even the hotel room.

"What hotel room?" I stammer. I realize in all our conversations it's not something I even considered. Now I'm dizzy at the thought.

"We need to sleep somewhere, Nick. Don't pee your pants, I'll get us separate rooms."

A week and a half before we're set to leave, Scooter goes into the hospital. The siren wakes us in the middle of the night.

I stare out my bedroom window with Jeremy and watch Mom stand with MaeLynn in the red flashing glow of the ambulance lights, as they wheel Scooter out and lift him into the back. He's sitting up, which is a good sign, an oxygen mask covering his face. Mom waits there while MaeLynn climbs inside and the doors close, and the siren starts up again, and it disappears, blaring through the night. Even when it's gone and it's dark and quiet again, she just stands there in MaeLynn's driveway.

"I wish Dad was here," I say.

"He's a chickenshit," Jeremy says, and I'm really too tired to argue.

When Mom comes back inside she tells us that Scooter had a small stroke, which is common for kids with progeria. This time, though, Scooter seemed lucky. It seemed he'd make it back home.

"Why did they take him then?" I ask.

"Precaution. Evaluation," she says, nudging me back to bed.

When I wake up, the first thing I do is call Jaycee. I'm still in my pajamas. She listens in silence as I tell her the details; everything that Mom told me.

"Do you think we'll have time?" she says.

"I hope so."

"We gotta find him, Nick. Really. We just gotta find his dad for him."

"We'll try," I say. "That's all we can do."

"Try not, or do not," she says. I roll my eyes. She's trying to quote Yoda. I just didn't recognize it her way.

"That's true, Jaycee. 'Try not. Do. Or do not.' There definitely is no try."

By the time I get home from school, the Scoot is back home too. I've never been so happy to see him.

"Hey, Scooter? How about a movie?" I yell to him where he sits on the swing on his stoop.

"Episode Five," he calls back.

74

I run up to my room and open my closet and start to dig around. I know what I need to find, and I'm pretty sure it's somewhere inside. I unload practically the whole closet before my hand feels it wedged way in the back. I pull it out. My Master Replicas Yoda Force FX lightsaber. How badly I had wanted it when I got it. My tenth birthday. Now I haven't touched it in years.

I press the switch and it powers on. The light whizzes up, making it glow an intense electric green. I stare at it for a minute, then close my eyes and pray.

I pray for Dad to come home and for Scooter to live, and for us to find his father. And for life to just go back to normal. Then I slash it about in the air for a bit in a halfhearted duel against evil. When I'm done, I grab a handful of Oreos and head on over to the Scoot's.

By the time I get there, he already has the movie on. He knows it doesn't matter if he starts without me—we've seen them all like four hundred times. He's on the living room couch, his feet sticking out, covered in an old crocheted blanket. He looks up and smiles when I come in.

He doesn't look great, which, for Scooter, is really saying something.

"How are you doing?" I ask, the lightsaber held behind my back.

"Okay," he says. "Small stroke. It's to be expected. Better that it wasn't my heart, though that will be next, I'm sure. But for now, it was a good thing."

"I'm sorry, Scooter," I say. "I'm worried for you."

"Don't be." He mutes the sound on the TV. "You know, Nick, 'always in motion is the future.'" He nods at Yoda, whose face is frozen on the screen.

"Yeah, I know," I say. "Speaking of which, I have something for you." I pull out the lightsaber and hold it out to him. "I want you to have it." I press the switch to make it glow. "May the force be with you, Scooter."

He laughs. "Wow, that's corny," he says.

But he takes it and rests it in his lap, closes his eyes, and runs his small hands up and down its blade. "Thanks, Nick, that's nice. It means a lot to me."

"Sure," I say.

"'A Jedi's strength flows from the Force,' right?"

"Right, Scooter."

He smiles. "Equally corny," he says.

10

On the bus to Rochester, Jaycee announces she's reading *Of Mice and Men* to me.

"Seriously, Nick," she says, slipping the book from its purple pouch and resting it in her lap, "it's the saddest, most beautiful story. Poor Lennie, wait till you see." I nod. "You'll have to read it in English lit this year anyway," she adds, "so I'm just saving you the trouble."

I don't argue, even though having a fifteen-thousand-dollar book out in the open on a bus makes me nervous. Plus, I'm not really in the mood for sad. She wants to do it, so I don't say that either.

We've been on the bus for a half hour. Neither of us has said too much since the Trailways station, so I'm cool with her reading. She turns to the first page and says, "Okay, here we go," and starts from the beginning. While she reads, I watch scenery go by out my window.

"'A few miles south of Soledad, the Salinas River drops in close to the hillside bank and runs deep and green.'" She pauses, says, "Soledad—that's in California. It's like the 1930s during the time of the Great Depression." Suddenly, she swats at my back. "You're not even listening to me, Nick."

"Yes, I am," I answer. "The banks are deep and green."

"Okay, well, then you are, sort of. So let me give you a little background. Lennie and George, the main characters, are these poor migrant farmworkers. They're looking for work on a ranch. They're on the road, like us." She perks up and adds, "And Lennie's retarded, like you are." She laughs at her own joke.

I smile despite myself. I love Jaycee. I'm glad to be with her. I mean this mostly in a "friend" way. What I really mean is, I'm not so happy at the moment, but I'm happier to be here with Jaycee.

"Just so you know," she continues, "the whole story takes place pretty much over one weekend, which is weird when you think about it because you feel like you know Lennie and George so well by the end.

"Anyway, George and Lennie are going to look for new work. But Lennie's hard to manage. He's really big and strong and doesn't know his own strength, so he's always accidentally hurting things, or killing them, with his bare hands. Like the small field mice he likes to pick up and stroke, because they're soft and furry and he's slow and all."

"Is that why it's called *Of Mice and Men?*" I ask.

"Oh, sort of," she answers. "I mean, not really. I'll tell you all that later. So anyway, Lennie is clumsy and unintentionally dangerous, so George tries to protect him, but he can't. And Lennie is always trying to get a hold of small, fluffy things."

"Like mice," I say, so she knows I'm paying attention.

"Yeah, like mice and rabbits and puppies. He wants a puppy really bad. Well, you'll see. You're going to meet them soon."

"Okay," I answer. I lean my head back against the window and listen.

" 'The water is warm too, for it has slipped twinkling over the yellow sands in the sunlight before reaching the narrow pool.' Isn't that beautiful?" she says.

I think it's a little boring, but I nod anyway, so she doesn't hit me. The truth is, even if it is boring, I don't mind listening because I'm not really in the mood to talk.

Actually, I haven't really wanted to talk much ever since the Scoot died. Which is nearly a week ago today.

Another stroke, they said. Or maybe it was his heart. In the end, I guess it doesn't matter. He went quietly in his sleep. MaeLynn said he didn't suffer.

The day after Scooter died, MaeLynn had a small funeral, and the day after that she put up a FOR SALE sign on her house. She said there was really nothing for her in Glenbrook anymore. Not now. Not without the Scoot. She said that

79

everything she had done was for that kid, and now she just needed to take some time to figure out her own life, to figure out what to do next.

"Yes, well," Mom had said, "there's a lot of that going on."

At the funeral, nearly the whole school showed up, which was really something, not to mention people from all over town. It surprised me just how many people actually cared about the Scoot. He was just like that, I guess. You never knew who he knew, or exactly what he was up to.

During the ceremony I kept looking for a man who might be Scooter's dad. I had seen an old photo that Scooter had given Jaycee, so I thought maybe I would recognize someone. Part of me was sure he would come. Part of me wanted to believe that. Also, I kept looking for my dad.

I actually couldn't believe that Dad didn't come home for the funeral, to say a final goodbye to the Scoot. But MaeLynn said that Scooter knew just how Dad felt about him, and that, in the scheme of things, a lifetime of hellos meant way more than one last little goodbye. Besides, MaeLynn said, after Scooter's first stroke she had talked to Dad and told him to keep doing what he was doing, and that Scooter had wanted the same. That he had this great opportunity to work on this big election story in New York City, and needed to stay on it. That he could mourn Scooter's death his own way, right from the spot he was in.

It surprised me a little that MaeLynn knew so much stuff about Dad. I mean, I hadn't talked to him once. And I still hadn't read his e-mails. Of course, Mom had filled me in some, to the extent that I wanted to listen. Which wasn't that much, I guess. Anyway, I was glad Dad had talked to MaeLynn and knew everything that had happened.

The hardest part of the funeral was when we had to walk up to the casket and pay our final respects. Even though I knew how small Scooter was, I hadn't thought about how tiny the casket would be. It was built for a toddler, and when I saw that, it was pretty hard not to cry.

Jaycee stayed with me the whole time. Neither of us had ever seen a dead body, and I was worried about how that might be. Mom said we didn't need to go up, but I wanted to see Scooter, or maybe I needed to, to believe he was really there. Jaycee held tight to my sleeve, and we walked up together.

And there he was, just lying there sort of fake-looking, like a weird old plastic doll. Honestly, it didn't seem like Scooter at all.

"Nick!" Jaycee whispered, tugging at my sleeve and nodding with her chin toward his body. I followed her gaze until I saw it there, nestled alongside him. My lightsaber. It was nearly as tall as he was. It was impossible, then, not to cry.

"I hope it's okay, Nick?"

I turned around to see MaeLynn.

"I probably should have asked you first. But you meant so much to him."

I nodded to let her know it was okay, since I couldn't get out any words.

81

MaeLynn talked briefly at the service. She said that Scooter was content in his life, that he knew he only had a short time on this earth, and that he had completely enjoyed himself while he was here. She said he was grateful for his friends.

She told us privately after, Jaycee and me, that Scooter wouldn't want us to be sad. That what he wanted most for everyone was for us to be happy, and to live big. To not fear change, or be afraid to take some risks.

As soon as MaeLynn was out of earshot, Jaycee said that what she said was a sign. A sign from Scooter that we still needed to go find his dad. As much as I didn't want to agree with her—that I had half hoped, now that Scooter was gone, that there was really no reason to go to Rochester—I knew that she was right.

"Okay," I said. She turned and looked at me, her eyes shiny with tears.

"Well, that's good, because I promised him we would."

"What? I thought we agreed not to tell him! I thought you didn't want to get his hopes up."

"I didn't. But after the stroke, well, I just wanted him to be sure."

"Oh," I said calmly, even though my heart was racing and I was suddenly feeling panicked inside. "But what if we *can't* find him, Jaycee? What if we don't?" How could she promise something to the Scoot that we might not be able to deliver on?

"It doesn't matter," she answered. "What matters is that the Scoot knows we cared enough to try."

"What happened to Yoda? Remember, 'Do. Or do not. There is no try'?"

"No worries," she said, resting her head on my shoulder, "he's just a dumb old puppet, loosely modeled on Einstein."

" 'The little man jerked down the brim of his hat and scowled over at Lennie. "So you forgot that awready, did you? I gotta tell you again, do I? Jesus Christ, you're a crazy bastard!" ' "

Jaycee shakes me and I jerk my head around. "Wait! What? What did I do?"

I've fallen asleep, that's what. There's drool on my cheek, and a smudge mark on the window. I wipe my face and try to figure out why Jaycee's calling me a bastard.

"Not you," she says without me asking. "That's George talking. He's mad at Lennie because he already forgot where they're going. I told you you weren't paying attention."

"I'm sorry," I say. "I guess I fell asleep. I was thinking about Scooter . . . and we did get up kind of early."

"It's okay." She pats my shoulder. "Go to sleep, my little Lennie."

When I wake up again, the bus is more crowded than before. I turn to Jaycee, but she's asleep now. She's got the hood on her green sweatshirt pulled up like always, a neon-green-haired troll doll hanging from a string around her neck. I hadn't noticed that one this morning. Her mouth is open and she's snoring a little.

I watch her chest go up and down as she breathes. No matter how I try, I can't really believe I'm on a bus to Rochester with Jaycee Amato.

As much as we talked and planned, I don't think I really thought we would go. Not until this morning when the alarm on my cell phone rang at 5:10 a.m., muffled from under my pillow, where I had stuck it so Mom wouldn't hear.

I tiptoed downstairs to use the first-floor shower, my heart pounding so hard I was sure she would hear *that*, then started back up to my room. Mom was waiting at the top of the stairs.

"Nicholas! Where are you going so early?"

I ran through everything Jaycee and I had rehearsed. "Extra help, remember? For science. I'm meeting Ryan." I said it impatiently, like I was annoyed she'd already forgotten the seed I had so carefully planted just a few days before. "I'm staying at his house this weekend. We have this huge science lab we have to get done, and he's way better at that stuff than I am."

She eyed me suspiciously for a second then said, "Okay, whatever you need to do. I'm in Philly, though, so make sure your brother knows where you are."

I smiled, because of course I knew she'd be in Philly, because that was all part of our plan.

Back in my room, I quickly threw on jeans, sneakers, a T-shirt and a hoodie, then emptied my backpack and filled it with crucial things. Deodorant, two more T-shirts, a toothbrush, boxers, and a pair of gym shorts to sleep in. I couldn't fit much more without it looking too bulky. Then I grabbed my cell, a message from Jaycee already blinking.

"Hey. U ready? Edge of Watson and Church in 20. Taxi will be there."

"I'll b there," I texted back, flying out the front door.

Outside, it was still dark, just on the verge of daylight, which was weird, since I never get up so early. I ran down Carver and crossed Main, then decided I had better cut through the back streets the rest of the way to the park. Just in case Mom drove by.

As the water tower came into view over the treetops, I couldn't help but think of Scooter, how he pretty much saved my life there. And at that moment, I knew I was doing the right thing. I owed it to Scooter to try to find his dad. It was the least I could do for the kid.

When I reached the Old West church on the corner of Watson, I glanced around but no taxi yet. And no Jaycee. I put my head down, hands on knees, and breathed. I must have run pretty fast. For one second, I thought about turning back, getting into bed, pulling the covers up over my head, and going to school like normal when the alarm clock rang again. But I wouldn't do that. Not to Scooter, or to Jaycee.

I reshouldered my backpack and walked toward the curb. From there, I could see her headed toward me in her green sweatshirt and bright orange high-top Converse sneakers.

"No taxi," I said when she reached me.

"We've got time. It'll be here." I nodded. "Everything go okay?"

"Like clockwork, you?"

She nodded too, and we stood on the corner, waiting, until the taxi pulled up, which only took another minute. I reached down for Jaycee's bag, but it was heavy, like she had a dead body in there.

"Jeez, Jaycee, what are you bringing?"

"You got an issue?" she said.

In the taxi, we were both pretty quiet. I pulled out the copy of Scooter's letter to his dad, just to make sure it was there, then found the small bunch of notes we had made and rifled through those. There wasn't much, mostly the one address in Rochester. *A. Reyland, 3625 First Street.*

I slipped it all back in and put my backpack down on the seat next to me.

"So," I finally asked, "do you really think we'll find him, Jaycee?" She kept her head turned out the window, didn't look at me.

"Don't know, Nick. The dude's a ghost," she said.

Now, I watch her sleep and wonder if she's worried that we won't actually find Scooter's dad. She always seems so confident. It's hard to know exactly what she's thinking.

I glance down. The book is still in her lap. *Of Mice and Men*, John Steinbeck. I pick it up and open it. She's put a Post-it on the corner of page 4. I find the words "crazy bastard" and laugh. I guess I didn't stay awake too long. I flip the book to its back cover and read:

They are an unlikely pair: George is "small and quick and dark of face"; Lennie, a man of tremendous size, has the mind of a young child. Yet they have formed a "family," clinging together in the face of loneliness and alienation.

I slip the book back into its pouch and into her bag and squeeze past her into the aisle. My legs are stiff from sitting so long. I walk to the front of the bus and ask the driver, a guy who looks around my dad's age and almost as fat, how long till we get to Rochester.

"About an hour," he says.

I go to the cubbyhole excuse for a bathroom and do my business, watch it disappear into the dark blue liquid that fills the toilet. There's something enjoyably challenging about taking a leak in a moving vehicle. After I'm done, I turn around and inspect myself in the small mirror.

Almost fifteen and in high school, and not a single impressive sign of puberty.

Sure I have a cheesy shadow of fuzz on my upper lip, but most of my friends are shaving. And as for down there, well, you don't want to know what's going on down there. Or what's *not* going on, I should say.

I suddenly find myself wondering if there's any chance that

Jaycee likes me, or if she just considers me a friend. I don't know why I'm thinking about this now, on this bus, in this bathroom. The truth is I haven't thought about it much before here. But now, here, I am.

I head back to our seats. Jaycee is awake, digging for something in her backpack.

"Hey," I say, "we've got like an hour left till Rochester."

"I know," she says. She turns her cell phone out to face me, then goes back to searching in her bag.

"Where'd you go? Bathroom?"

"Yeah."

"How bad?"

"Not too bad." I squeeze in past her. She's pulled the book back out plus a pack of Juicy Fruit. She offers a stick to me and I take it. She puts it back in her bag, then puts her hand down, resting on my knee. My ears burn red. I don't know how I can feel sad and excited both at the same time.

I mean, here I am missing the Scoot, and then, all I can think about is kissing Jaycee. About what it would feel like to touch my lips to hers for a second. Whether she'd like it, or whether she'd be mad. My heart pounds loud enough that I'm sure she can hear it. My hands go sweaty. I glance sideways to see if she can tell, and sure enough, she's staring at me.

I look down. "Want to read more *Of Mice and Men* to me?" I'm doing my best to keep my voice normal with her staring, hand on my leg.

"Sure," she says. She opens the book to the page she was on, then turns to me with her crazy-amazing eyes and laughs. "I mean, if you're not gonna kiss me, that is."

My whole face goes red. I can't believe she's read my mind that way.

"Well, duh," she says, slouching, her knees bent and pressed up against the seat in front of us. She starts to read again.

By the time we pass the WELCOME TO ROCHESTER sign, George and Lennie are at the ranch where they meet Slim and Candy and Curly. Candy is this old guy with one hand who has a crippled old dog that stinks, so the other ranchers want to kill it. To put it out of its misery and all. Curly is the boss's son, a real jerk who tries to egg Lennie on. George tells Lennie over and over that, no matter what, he shouldn't mess with Curly, or worse, Curly's wife, who the men all think is a whore. So George tells Lennie to stay away from her, and that if he doesn't, he won't get to tend the rabbits when they finally get their own ranch. As soon as he tells Lennie this, you know there's going to be trouble. Which is why I keep wondering what Jaycee likes about the book. I say this to her, before she can read my mind.

"It's foreshadowing," she says. "Haven't you heard of foreshadowing?" She shakes her head like I'm thick or something.

"Yeah, I know what foreshadowing is, Jaycee. But it still seems sad to me."

"I guess. But that's what makes it so brilliant. Because, if I closed the book now, you'd want to know what happens, right? Sure, you know something's going to happen, but you don't know what. And you care about them, so you want to know."

The truth is, I don't know how much I really care what happens. In fact, I don't even know how I've been paying attention at all. Because ever since Jaycee's comment about the kiss, it's been almost impossible to concentrate. I mean, how am I supposed to do that, just start kissing her, in the middle of a crowded bus to Rochester?

Then again, how do I do that alone in a hotel room, with a bed, which is where we'll be in about a half hour?

So half the time I'm listening to her read—or at least trying to—and the other half I'm busy thinking about kissing her and sleeping in a hotel instead of paying attention. So I have to keep stopping to ask questions so I can pretend to understand.

"So, the gist is, they're gonna work on this farm until they save enough money to buy their own ranch, right?" I ask. "Then Lennie can have the rabbits and they'll all live happily ever after? But then they meet Curly's wife, and we all know that there's no way that's ever gonna happen?"

"Basically," Jaycee says. "If oversimplified."

She's about to start reading again, but the bus makes a wide sweeping turn and pulls into the next station.

"Rochester!" the driver yells as the bus stops, its air brakes hissing as it settles lower to let us all out. Jaycee puts the book in its pouch and into her backpack, zips it up, slings it over her shoulder, and stands.

"Well, this is it, Lennie," she says. "Four days and one lead. And there is no try. So we'd better find a way to make this happen."

Then she grabs my arm and pulls me behind her, and we head down the steps into the bright unknown of Rochester.

11

We clear the bus fumes, and I wait for Jaycee to tell me what's next on our plan. She kneels behind me searching through that heavy backpack of hers. I open my cell phone. It's nearly eleven-thirty. We've been traveling in the gray, airless bus for almost five hours, but it actually feels longer to me. I have to squint against the bright sunlight.

Jaycee balances her backpack on her knee, rummages, and pulls out some fat book which she wedges under her arm, then goes back to searching again. Satisfied, she zips and re-shoulders her pack, and we stand there in silence, me waiting for her instructions and Jaycee tapping the book against her thigh as she scans our surroundings.

I realize now, standing here like this, that during the whole bus ride, we managed not to discuss anything to do with the Scoot or our plan, or how to find his dad. Instead, except for when I slept, Jaycee read to me nearly the entire time.

Even though I don't love the book, I do like listening to

Jaycee read. I like her voice, and how she changes it to get across the different characters and moods of the story. It's not like she tries to imitate them, but somehow she makes them come alive and the words sound mostly interesting.

"So, now what?" I ask finally, when it seems like we might just keep standing here.

"Hold your horses," she says, "I'm thinking."

She puts the book between her legs, cups her hands to her eyes, and looks around, then opens the book and pulls out a large AAA foldout map from a pocket in the back. She hands the book to me. It's called *A Weekender's Guide to Rochester* and has all sorts of yellow and pink Post-it notes stuck to it.

"You brought maps and books?" I ask.

She frowns. "Like, duh. I'm not an idiot."

It stings a little. Obviously, this means that I am. And she's right, of course. I should have thought of that.

"Well, what about a compass and a protractor?" I say, then laugh because I may be useless, but I'm funny.

"As a matter of fact, I'll do you one better." She digs inside her bag again then says, "Voilà!" and waves a small gray box at me.

"You did not!" I shove her affectionately. She's got a GPS in her hand.

"And charger," she says proudly, pulling out a black cord with her other hand. "It's the Doofus's. He's got like fifty of these because one is not enough. He won't even notice it's gone."

93

While Jaycee fiddles with the GPS, I page through the travel book so it seems like I'm doing something worthwhile. The truth is I have no idea what to do and no idea what I'm looking for. I can't even believe I'm standing here in Rochester. I glance around for anything I can see that might be helpful, and that's when I see it, across the main highway, rising from the center of a small cluster of office buildings. A big blue trapezoidal water tower. I hadn't noticed it at first, but now I can't take my eyes off it. I mean, any old water tower, sure. But a blue one that looks like an AT-AT Walker? It seems like a weird coincidence.

I don't bother to say anything to Jaycee. I mean, how will that fact help us? She'll just say something that makes me feel dumb. I keep scanning for something more useful.

To our left, the street sign reads East Broad Street, and behind me is Chestnut. In front of us, the large intersection reads Clinton Avenue. Across Clinton, a busy main road, is a gas station, a diner, a KFC, and a Dunkin' Donuts, and beyond that, a Best Western hotel.

A hotel.

Now maybe I can help. I'm just about to point it out when she says, "Okay, how about we go to the hotel and get settled. Change and pee, and get ourselves something to eat."

"How about there?" I blurt, pointing toward the Best Western. Jaycee looks, then busts out laughing.

"What?"

94

"We're staying at the Sheraton on South Avenue, Nick. Don't you think I already made us reservations?" She turns the GPS to me and shows me a map with a thick blue line illustrating our route from where we stand to a red star marking the Sheraton Four Points Hotel. Right to the door, practically. I nod, embarrassed for a change.

"It's not that close, but we can still walk it, I think," she says, nudging me to move.

As we walk, I wonder how she knew how to do all this stuff, bring the right things, and book us at that hotel.

"The Doofus stays there on business," she says, doing that crazy mind-reading thing. "There's a News 10 affiliate station downtown. And he's got an expense account," she adds, "which made it easy. I just registered online, got a printed copy. All I have to do is flash the confirmation. They won't even know I'm not with him."

"Because I look just like J.P.," I say sarcastically.

"Thank God, no." She laughs. "Don't worry, you'll stay back. They won't find out, believe me." She moves her backpack to her other shoulder and pulls me next to her and starts to walk again. "Trust me, Lennie. I've got it all under control."

We crisscross the streets of Rochester, the GPS lady talking to us in a British accent from inside Jaycee's front pocket. It amazes me how comfortable Jaycee is, as if she knows the place—like she's grown up here. I feel like a dope as I stumble along beside her.

"You know, it's no big deal, Nick, really," she says, smiling at me. "You grow up in Manhattan, and nothing really intimidates you anymore. Especially with no parents. Or at least no dad for real, and no mom, effectively."

"What do you mean?" The few times I've met her mom she's seemed nice enough, even if she looks a little country club.

"I told you," Jaycee says, "she's a total social butterfly. Always has been. She'd rather play tennis or go out to dinner than sit around doing homework with her kid. Trust me. I rode a city bus to school alone by the time I was eight years old. Maybe seven."

"It can't be that bad," I say, trying to keep pace with her. "I saw her make spaghetti and meatballs."

"Aberration," she says. "Put it this way. Yesterday, when I told her I was sleeping at a girlfriend's this weekend, she didn't even ask which one. Even though I left on a Thursday. As long as it was a female, she was okay. Having nothing to do with the fact that she has some big news gala with the Doofus this weekend and probably needs to shop for new dresses."

She tries to sound light about it, but I feel a little bad for her. I mean, at least my mom cares where I'm going. She knows Ryan pretty well; she wouldn't let me go off just anywhere. And she'd be pissed if she knew that I lied. I take a few large strides to catch up with her again, so that we're walking shoulder to shoulder. This close, in the crisp, fresh air, I can smell the shampoo in her hair.

96

"That's better," she says, slinging her arm over my shoulder like we're best buds.

"Man, Jaycee," I say, trying not to pay too much attention to her arm around me, "you seriously thought of everything. You did a really good job with the plans." I'm being sincere. She may think it's easy, but it totally impresses me.

She stops and turns to me, her eyes a crazy cool blue in the bright sun. "Who cares, Nick?" she says. "You can never count on them anyway."

"Count on what?"

"On plans. I'm just saying. So you might as well not work too hard to make them, because you really can't count on them at all."

"Oh," I say, sounding as confused as I am. "Why?"

She shrugs and starts to walk again.

"I don't know. Ask Steinbeck. It's from the book." She pulls the GPS out and glances at it, then shoves it back in her pocket. "Well, from the poem that the book is named after, really. 'To a Mouse,' by Robert Burns, 1785."

I nod like I get it, but I don't, which, apparently, she senses.

"Of Mice and Men," she cues me. "You know, '. . . the best laid plans of mice and men go oft awry'? That's why the book is called that, by the way. You asked before, so I'm telling you. That line is from a poem. It really just means that plans fail. They get messed up. 'Go oft awry.' It's a line from the Burns poem. Well sort of, but not exactly. Actually, the translation

97

to English is 'the best laid plans go oft awry,' but that's not what the real poem says."

I nod again, doing my best to follow.

"The real poem is Scottish," she clarifies. "But anyway, the point is, it just means that even carefully made plans get messed up." She glances at me.

"I get it," I say.

She busts out laughing. "No you don't," she says.

I'm about to argue, but she stops and tips my chin up to look in front of us. We're standing across the street from the Sheraton Four Points Hotel.

"Come on, Lennie, we're here," she says, pulling me toward the entrance.

Inside, the hotel is pretty fancy. Jaycee directs me to the back of the lobby near the elevators, then checks us in without a hitch. Like she's a hotel pro or something.

"Get the look off your face," she says, waving the room key proudly in the air. "I told you it'd be easy. I just said I was his daughter and that the Doofus was parking the car."

She hands me the plastic card that you swipe in the slot in the door. It makes me think of Mom because, when we travel, she always says how she misses the real keys. The metal kind they used to have, big brass things with weight that felt good in your hand. Mom says everything is plastic now, and sighs when she says it, as if she's a hundred years old. Still, the key makes me think of her and miss her a little, and wonder about my dad.

As we ride the elevator to the sixth floor, I look at the key and panic and maybe my face goes white or something, because Jaycee holds up a second plastic card and laughs. "No worries, goofball, I told you I'd get us separate rooms."

The elevator opens, and I follow her down the hall. She stops at room 619 and swipes the card and walks in. I stand in the hall waiting as the door closes behind her. She immediately opens it again.

"Oh, not separate, exactly." She nods at the door right next to it. "They're adjoining. That's yours. But you can come through here." She pulls me inside, then faces me to a door between the rooms, held open by a rubber doorstop. "See, it opens and closes and *locks* and everything, but we're connected like twins in the middle."

I roll my eyes at her sarcasm, but my heart races and I start to sweat a bit. I mean, it's weird enough to walk into a hotel room without my family to begin with. I feel like an imposter, or like I'm on some secret mission, which now that I think about it, I guess, sort of, I am. *But still. To be in a hotel room with Jaycee?*

Jaycee laughs, nudges me into my side, then steps exaggeratedly back into hers and closes the door. She knocks. I open the door, and she busts out laughing.

"Oh brother," I say.

"Okay, seriously, I'm going to freshen up," she says when she's done being hilarious, then closes the door again.

I stand there for a few seconds, then sit on the end of my bed, toss my backpack down, and close my eyes and think. *Now what? I mean, what on earth am I doing here?*

I turn on the television and find some local news. They're going on about the teams in the World Series, about how the series is being played so late in the year. I'm not a huge baseball fan so I don't really care that much. Plus, it occurs to me that if I watch long enough Jaycee's stepdad could appear on the screen, which would totally weird me out.

I leave the TV and head into the bathroom. It's sparkling clean and bright. There's a marble counter and fluffy towels and those tiny bottles of shampoo that Mom is always oohing at and taking home in her bag. Like what's so great about a little bottle of shampoo?

I take a leak and stare at myself in the mirror for the second time today, trying to get a grip on the things that have happened so far:

1. My dad has left. According to Jeremy, this is for good, but Jeremy is an idiot and I don't know who would listen to him in the first place.

2. Scooter is dead. This seems impossible even though I knew it was going to happen. The Scoot has been my next-door neighbor for as long as I can remember, and pretty much my best friend. Scooter is dead. Scooter is

100

dead. I say it two more times in my head to see if I can get it to settle.

3. MaeLynn is selling the house and leaving, so even she won't be there anymore. She's been the one person that always makes Dad laugh.

4. I am in a hotel in Rochester with Jaycee Amato and think I may want to kiss her. And I think that she may want me to. No one knows I am here, and Mom would probably kill me if she did.

5. We've promised to find Scooter's dad and deliver a fifteen-thousand-dollar book, and I sure as hell hope that we can.

I turn off the lights, head back into the room, and knock softly on the door to Jaycee's side. *No answer.* Maybe she's in the bathroom.

I go back and sit, stare at the TV and wait. A few minutes later, I tap on her door again.

No answer.

I turn the knob. It's unlocked. So I open it a crack and peer in.

Jaycee is straight ahead, face-planted down on her bed.

I shake my head at the sight of her. The girl is totally nuts. She's all hurry up and go, then sound asleep on the job. I guess she must be exhausted. But I'm waking her anyway, because after all, this was her dumb idea. She's the one who insisted. She's the one who came up with this ridiculous plan.

I stand at the door for another minute watching her sleep, then push it open and walk in. She's definitely asleep, breathing heavy, her long black pigtails flat on her pillow over her head like donkey ears.

Her cell phone is on the nightstand. Next to her, her backpack is spilled open, its contents spread out on the bed:

- The Rochester travel book with Post-it notes;
- Scooter's copy of *Of Mice and Men*;
- A jar of peanut butter and plastic knife;
- A pair of green Marshall J. Freeman sweatpants, a few T-shirts, and some unmentionables poking out;
- The GPS and a bunch of chargers;
- More troll doll necklaces, neon-pink, rainbow, and blue hair;
- Four Slinkys. Two metal (one original silver and one fancy gold), and two plastic ones (both rainbow-colored); and
- A yo-yo and a few colored elastic bands for her hair.

The girl sure knows how to pack.

I decide she's asleep for a while, go back to my room and find a pad and pen. I write a note that says, "Going exploring. Maybe I'll find some clue. Text me when you wake up." I put it on her nightstand then head out into the hotel to see what I can find.

Downstairs, the lobby is quiet. Beyond the lobby there's

a gift shop and a small sports bar / restaurant. As I walk past it, the smell of French fries makes my stomach rumble. I have a few bucks in my pocket and think about getting some, but then figure I should wait for Jaycee.

I wander down a long corridor past a large meeting room, then a gym, and an indoor pool. The smell of chlorine is strong. I half wish I'd thought to bring swim trunks with me. Next to the pool is a lame sort of game room, with a beat-up billiard table, a Ping-Pong table, and some older video games. There's also a vending machine, which is a godsend. I put a dollar in and press L9 and a Rice Krispies treat plunks out. I put a few more dollars in the change machine and get myself a bunch of quarters. I play two games of Need for Speed, then head back through the lobby.

Near the elevators, I pass a row of pay phones and find a Rochester White Pages in one of the cubbyholes. I flip to the R's and search for Reyland, but the only one listed is the same old A. Reyland on First Street. I flip to the front cover—it's current—then back to the R's. Not a single other Reyland. I mean, didn't Jaycee say he grew up here? He must have family, so where are they? Have they all just disappeared? Are there really no other Reylands in Rochester? For some reason, all those R's sound funny in my head, and a Dr. Seuss sort of rhyme starts to form as I head back to our rooms.

Are the Reylands really rare?
If I find them will they care?

103

Do they wear their underwear?

In Rochester.

I think it's pretty good, so I decide I'll have to share it with Jaycee. Plus, she'll improve it when she hears it, I'm sure.

Back in my room I put my backpack down, then tap softly on the door between us. No answer.

Crap.

I push the door open again and peek in. Jaycee's not in the bed anymore.

I call her name. She answers from the bathroom, says she's not really feeling too well. I go back to my side and sit on the bed. Suddenly, I'm anxious for home.

I walk back into her room and tap on the bathroom door.

"Hey, you want me to get you something?"

"Some ginger ale?" she calls back. "If you can find any."

I walk to the end of the hall toward the elevators, to look for the sign to the ice machine. I figure there'll be a soda vending machine there as well.

As a kid, I loved the hotel ice machines and was always fighting with Jeremy over whose turn it was to fill the bucket. "Dump it!" Dad would say. "For Christ's sake, it's free! Just dump it and take turns." I can remember the exact feeling of trekking down the hotel corridor in my pajamas, alone late at night, my parents' door wedged slightly open with Dad's shoe. I guess it was one of those first sharp steps toward independence.

I find the ice machine, and I'm right because there's a soda machine across from it. I dig in my pocket for some quarters then scan down the glass window. Coke, Diet Coke, Sprite, Tropicana Orange Juice, Grape Hi-C, and three different slots with bottled waters, but no ginger ale. I'm about to pick Sprite when I see it there. I don't know how I missed it the first time. Second from the bottom in the corner. A Cherry RC Cola.

I mean, who can resist? I buy two and a Sprite and head back to the room.

Jaycee is back on the bed again, this time faceup, her head propped on her pillow, her hood up over her head. She doesn't look so great.

"No ginger ale," I say, holding a can out toward her. "Cherry cola or Sprite?" She points to the Sprite, pops the lid, and drinks. "You okay?" I ask.

"Yeah, a little queasy. Maybe I need to eat something. I'm probably just tired. But we should get going already." She grabs her cell phone and turns it to face me like I can possibly see it from here. "It's already after one," she says.

"Hey, I've been ready since we got here. And where are we going anyway? I mean, do you actually have any idea?"

"Yeah, I figure we'll start stalking some Reylands." She leans over and pulls open the nightstand drawers. "Maybe I can find a phone book . . ."

"Don't bother," I say. "I tried that already. White Pages in the lobby, but no one other than our infamous A. But we knew that already, Jaycee. It's not like we haven't been look-ing. I know you were expecting some miracle when we got here."

"Really?" she asks, deflated. "I guess you're right. But we'll find him. I'm sure we'll find him here."

She stands and starts gathering her stuff into her bag. I toss the two cherry colas in the minibar. When I walk back to the bed she hands the Steinbeck book to me, like I should hold on to it instead of her.

"It's just so weird, Nick," she says, looking at me with those eyes. "How can he not be anywhere?"

"Don't know. The dude's a ghost," I say.

12

We grab sandwiches at a deli, then Jaycee turns on the GPS and we start our trek toward First Street. We don't really know anything about the Reylands that supposedly live there. If they still do, that is. Like, whether they're even related to Guy Reyland or the Scoot. But it's the only lead we have, so we follow it. We turn right off of South Avenue and left on East Broad Street, then head southeast toward downtown Rochester.

The day is sunny and bright and, despite our cuckoo mission, I am content to be doing what I am doing. I mean, I'm happy to be away from home, away from Jeremy and Mom, on this mission with Jaycee. Even though I'm still not completely sure what it is.

Jaycee's pretty quiet for Jaycee. I get the sense she's still not feeling too well. I tap on her shoulder, figure it's time to cheer her up.

"You know," I say, "Reyland is a really rare name."

"I guess so," she says.

"Really rare, I mean."

She turns to me. "Your point?" She thinks I'm serious.

"Nothing. Just saying. Are the Reylands really rare?"

She cocks her head sideways, like maybe now she knows I'm up to something. I make a face, then say, "I'm just wondering. Are the Reylands really rare, will we find them anywhere? Are the Reylands really rare in Rochester?" She punches me. I laugh and keep going.

"Are the Reylands really rare, do they wear their underwear, in Rochester?"

"You're an idiot," she says.

"So, you do not really care, if the Reylands are so rare, in Rochester?"

She slaps me again, so I cut it. We walk for a block or so, and then she says, "If you're hungry, eat a pear, with the Reylands on a dare, but the Reylands never share, in Rochester."

I smile. "Will they catch a polar bear, in Rochester?"

Jaycee shakes her head then buzzes me out, "Enhhh!" like it's a game show. "No good," she says. "You left out the Reylands. I mean that was the whole point of it, Lennie. There have to be Reylands in there."

I roll my eyes. "It's *my* poem. And it would be great if you'd actually stop calling me Lennie."

We spend the rest of the walk rhyming with Reylands

until we reach the corner of First Street. The British lady announces our arrival—*"Turn right, First Street, you have reached your destination"*—from inside Jaycee's pocket. I glance at my cell. It's nearly two-thirty. We've been walking for more than an hour.

"This is it," she says. "You have the number?" I pull out the papers from my backpack.

"Yeah, I programmed it in, 3625." I nod toward the GPS in her pocket, proud of my contribution, then double-check the paper just in case.

"We can turn this off then." She reaches in to silence it, takes a deep breath, and looks up at me. "You've got the book, right?" I pat my backpack. She must be nervous—she handed it right to me, watched me put it in, back at the hotel. "Well then," she says, but neither of us moves.

Now that I can tell Jaycee's nervous, my heart pounds a little. I count on her to be the cool one. After all, this was *her* idea. I'm just an innocent bystander. Plus, I suddenly realize we haven't even talked about what we'll actually say if we do find Guy Reyland. Especially now that Scooter is dead.

"Don't worry. We'll figure it out," Jaycee says, even though I'm absolutely sure I didn't say anything out loud. She nudges me and we start walking slowly down First Street.

"But what if he's a total jerk who doesn't give a crap about his kid? He did leave him in the first place. And never called, or came back to see how he did."

"Maybe he couldn't. Maybe he wanted to, but didn't know how."

I snort. I want to believe her, that there can possibly be some good reason why Guy Reyland just up and disappeared. But even MaeLynn had said he was nothing but a coward and a jerk.

"You know, Nick, people grow up and change. Even adults. They improve themselves. Some people can change an awful lot in twelve years." She stops mid-block, hands on hips, and stares at me. "So let's just hope that he did."

I shrug and look around. The house we've stopped in front of is number 3420. It's a small, dumpy blue house with a rusted old Chevrolet parked in front. The yard is shabby and overgrown, and a bunch of kids' toys litter the lawn. A purple Hot Wheels rider. A red trike. A bunch of Wiffle ball bats and balls. I look up and down the street. It's not a great neighborhood, and the houses all look pretty much the same.

I think about what Jaycee has just said and wonder if it's really true. I mean, if Guy Reyland had changed that much, wouldn't he have come back looking for his son? But he hadn't. Not once. At least as far as I knew. In more than twelve years, he had never even called or checked in on the Scoot. So how much could he have changed? And judging from the neighborhood, if he lives here, there isn't much hope that he has.

Anyway, in my opinion, it wasn't just Guy Reyland. It was everyone. People seemed to get worse, not better, like they went in the opposite direction. They got less happy and less hopeful as they got older. Until they were fat and depressed and didn't give a crap about the world.

"I don't know, Jaycee. My dad, I'm telling you, he was this happy-go-lucky guy. A good job, a successful journalist, and now . . ." I stop there because I really don't know what my point was.

"And now *what?*"

"Well, you know. He just did pretty much nothing but lie on the couch anymore. I barely remember him the other way. The fun, not fat way, I mean."

"But, see, Nick. You make my point. He's changing things. He's walking. So you can't fault him now. He's trying to get better."

I shrug. "You know, my mom says he made it all the way to New York City. I didn't think he would, but he did. He's staying with some friend there who works for the *Daily News*. He's doing some freelance for them."

"See?" Jaycee says brightly. "People change. I bet everything gets better."

"I don't know." I glance down the block again. "Jeremy keeps saying that he's never coming back, that he misses the city and his freedom. What if he's right, Jaycee?"

"He's not." She wraps her arms tightly around herself and shivers. The sun has gone behind clouds and the air has grown noticeably cool.

"Come on," I say, tugging her sleeve. "Enough talk about stupid stuff, let's get this crazy thing done."

The house at 3625 First Avenue looks like all the others on the street. The yard's overgrown and the outside is in need of a paint job. It's supposed to be white, but it's the color of cement. In the driveway there's a beat-up red Dodge Ram and a baby blue Buick from another decade altogether. I look at Jaycee and she shrugs.

"If he lives here, he could use fifteen thousand dollars," she says. "You ready?" I nod. "Okay then."

She walks ahead to the front door, and I follow behind, my heart racing. On the stoop, to the right of the door, there's a mailbox, a fake-gold rectangular thing with a black eagle on it. She opens it.

"What are you doing!" I pull on her, but she elbows me away.

"Looking for names," she says. She reaches in. "Never mind. It's empty. Guess somebody is home." On cue, a figure passes through the living room, past a small TV and a bunch of plants in a curtained window. It's a woman. I think she sees us. She heads toward the door.

"You'd better ring the bell," I say.

Jaycee reaches out and presses. It makes a broken ring, and the woman peers out the narrow side window. Jaycee waves sweetly, and the door opens partway, and she eyes us through the screen.

"Yes?" She's about my mom's age, in jeans and a navy sweatshirt. Her hair is long and dark, streaked with blond, and pulled back in a ponytail. She has a cigarette in her hand. "Can I help you kids?" she says.

"We're looking for A. Reyland," Jaycee answers. "Or someone named Guy Reyland if he's here. We've been asked to give him something."

I don't know if it's because I'm nervous, or because Jaycee sounds like she's spouting lines from some really bad detective movie, but I laugh a little. I can't help it. The woman narrows her eyes at me and I turn my head to try to stop.

"I'm Arlene," she says. "Who's asking?" She takes a drag of her cigarette and blows smoke through the screen. "And give him what, why?"

"Just something for Guy. Do you know him, Guy Reyland? So we can give him the thing?" Now she's totally stammering. It's weird to hear her that way. Not that I could do better. "It's from his son," she tries adding. "His son asked us to deliver it to him." I'm having a hard time not laughing now. I mean, I'm trying not to, but I can't help it. Jaycee nudges me, and I put my head down.

A loud voice calls out, "What's going on, Arlene?" A tall, white-haired man in an undershirt and black slacks appears. He's an older guy, barrel-chested and red faced. And he has a freaking hunting rifle in his hand. "Damned troublemakers again?"

113

"Jesus," I say. I pull Jaycee back from the door.

"Just some kids horsing around," Arlene says to the man.

Jaycee glares at me. "Please," she says. "We're not horsing around or making trouble, I swear. We're just trying to find Guy Reyland. It's important. We're being serious here."

The guy gets a look on his face, cocks the rifle, aims it at the screen. "It's not even Halloween yet and you're all up to your pranks. I should shoot you now. Shut the door, Arlene."

"Wait!" Jaycee pleads. She yanks at my backpack frantically, like she's going to take the book out and show it to him.

"Are you crazy!" I push her hand away and grab her sleeve. "Let's just get out of here." I start to walk, pulling her with me, so the dude is clear that we're leaving. Jaycee looks back at the woman with pleading eyes.

"His kid just died. Really!"

"Ain't no one here named Guy, anyway," the woman says. She starts to close the door.

"Damned kids," the man yells, then slams it shut behind us.

We walk quietly back along First Street, the way we came. I get the feeling Jaycee's mad at me, and I feel bad, but I don't know what to say. We got what we came for. They told us there was no one named Guy Reyland there. And they didn't seem to know who he was. I wasn't about to get shot for it.

"He wasn't going to shoot us," Jaycee says. "And who even knows if they were telling the truth. Did you see how she looked at him? They were lying. It felt like they knew who he is."

"It's not a detective movie, Jaycee, with everyone hiding things," I say, wondering how she always knows exactly what I'm thinking. "If they knew, they would have said so. But maybe we should go back there. I mean, he only had a shotgun aimed at us. Maybe he'll invite us in for cookies."

She punches me, but the gesture doesn't carry any of her usual enthusiasm.

"Are you okay?" I ask.

"Just disappointed," she says.

"You know, even if they do know him and were lying for some reason, they didn't really seem like the best kind of relations. If those are his friends and family, maybe we don't want to find him. Or give him a fifteen-thousand-dollar book. Maybe we should just give it back to MaeLynn."

Jaycee stops and glares at me. "Scooter wanted this," she says. We walk another few blocks in silence before Jaycee speaks to me again.

"So, I know what Jeremy thinks, but what about you? Do you think your dad will come back?"

I look at her. "What?"

"Your dad. Do you think he's coming back?"

I think for a minute. Obviously, we're done talking about Guy Reyland.

"I don't know. He sends me notes. E-mails. But I don't

open them." I don't know why I tell her this now, but I do. Maybe so she knows that I trust her. I figure I'll just let her lecture me about how idiotic I am.

"Really?" is all she says.

"Yeah. Pretty much every day since he left. But I haven't read them."

"Why not?"

"Not sure. I think I'm mad. Or maybe I'm afraid what they'll say."

She turns and gives me sad, puppy-dog eyes. Only suddenly I realize that they're all red and glassy and she actually doesn't look too good. Plus, she's shivering.

I reach out and touch her forehead on impulse, like my mom's done to me a thousand times. She's burning up; it hurts when I touch her skin.

"Jaycee, you're freaking hot!" Her cheeks are bright red. I can't believe I didn't notice it before.

"I am?" She wraps her arms around herself. "I was thinking I didn't feel too well."

"Jeez," I say. "Why didn't you tell me? I'll get us a cab. Come on."

It takes me a few blocks, but I manage to flag down a taxi and push her in first, and we ride in silence, Jaycee leaning against me, shivering, all the way back to the hotel.

13

By the time we get up to the room, Jaycee is puking her brains out. Well actually, even before then. She pukes on the sidewalk when we get out of the cab; she pukes in the hotel lobby bathroom. And then she pukes in the wastebasket in my room before we make it into hers, which I'm sort of wishing she hadn't.

"Sorry," she squeaks.

"No problem," I say.

She spends another twenty minutes puking in the bathroom in her room. When she finally comes out, she gets into her bed and pulls the covers up.

"Man, I'm sick," she says. She looks terrible.

"I'll get you some ice," I say.

When I get back to the room, I wrap the ice in a washcloth and put it on the desk and bang it with the iron I find on a shelf in the closet. When it's crushed up sufficiently, I put it in a water glass and bring it to her. She's lying curled up on her side.

"Here." I hold out the glass to her.

"I can't," she says.

I shake it a little and make the ice chips rattle. "They're tiny. Take one little piece. Trust me. Seriously. I'm a fever expert."

She reaches out and takes a chip with her fingers. It melts away before she gets it to her mouth.

"Come on," I say. "Take another. Years of practice have finally led me to this moment." I'm trying to be funny—to reassure her—but I'm a little worried too. I mean, nobody knows better than I do that a little fever doesn't kill you. Then again, that's me. And I am not Jaycee. And she's been puking for at least a half hour and is really burning up. I hand her another ice chip, but she's tucked her arm back under the blanket. She looks at me with her bloodshot, husky-dog eyes, then opens her mouth like a baby bird. I'm self-conscious, but I drop it in.

"Thanks," she mumbles.

I watch her huddled under the blankets, shaking, for another few minutes, and try to decide what to do. "Hey, Jaycee, do you want me to call your mom?"

"No," she says. "God, no . . . She'll kill me." I can barely hear her.

"Are you sure?"

I wait, but she doesn't answer. She's out cold.

I sit on the edge of her bed, turn the TV on, and put the volume on mute. I flip channels a few times but there's really nothing on. I'm kind of hungry. I ate only half my sandwich earlier. I glance at the clock on the nightstand. It's nearly five. I think about ordering room service, but I don't want to wake Jaycee. Plus I'm guessing it's expensive.

I go to my room to get my wallet and am met by a nasty stench, then remember that Jaycee puked in my wastebasket. I pull the bag from it and tie it tightly with a knot. Good thing I'm used to puking. I find another plastic bag in the closet and put it inside that and tie it even tighter. I walk out into the hallway and find a garbage can near the elevators and dump it. By the time I get back to the room I'm not really hungry anymore.

I look in on Jaycee again. She's sound asleep, breath shallow and rapid. I can feel the heat radiate from her body through the blankets. I wonder vaguely if the hotel has a doctor but then decide it wouldn't. It's not a cruise ship, I mean. If I need to, I guess I can find a hospital. *If I need to.* I just really can't take anything happening to Jaycee. The Scoot was enough for me.

I lie on my back next to her, my legs hanging over the side, feet touching the floor. I pull out my cell phone. The background is a photo of Yoda that the Scoot put there weeks ago. It's so cheesy, I smile. I can't bring myself to change it. I look over at Jaycee again. *It's just a fever,* I reassure myself, and I know a few things about fevers. They come and they go. They're usually not a big deal. She'll be okay. She'll probably feel better in the morning. I hold the phone above my head and stare at Yoda and breathe.

By six-thirty, Jaycee is still burning up. I've been lying here forever just thinking about Scooter and everything, and listening to Jaycee sleep.

I get up from the bed and start to dial home. Jeremy should be there, although I don't know why I'm calling him. I make sure the door is unlocked and cross to my side of the room.

It rings four times before he picks up.

"Yeah?"

"Jeremy, it's Nick."

"I can see that," he says.

"Hey."

"Hey, what? I'm watching something here. What do you want?"

"Nothing. I'm just checking in."

"Where are you?" he asks. I wonder if he really cares or just knows he should ask. It is a school night, and I haven't come home all afternoon. Of course, for me it feels like a million years since I left. To him, it's probably nothing. I bet he hasn't even noticed.

"I'm at Ryan's," I say. "Doing homework. I think I'm just gonna sleep here."

"It's a school night," he says, which impresses me.

"So?"

"Okay then." He hangs up. So much for impressive. I throw my cell phone on the bed.

I walk around the room in circles, then sit and dig through my backpack for something, but there's really nothing in there. I don't even have a Slinky or yo-yo like Jaycee does.

I pick up my phone and dial Jeremy again.

"Jesus, what?" he answers.

"What?" I say.

"You just called me."

"I know," I say. I can't believe my brother. He's such a jerk. He doesn't give a crap about me. I should just hang up. Suddenly I feel like crying. "Jeremy, I'm not at Ryan's," I say.

"No? Where? The rich girl's?"

"Not exactly. Well, sort of."

"Great. Have fun." He hangs up again.

I dial him back.

"Seriously, dude," he says.

"I'm with Jaycee, but we're in Rochester," I blurt, before he can cut me off.

"What the heck?" I hear him shift and turn the TV volume down.

"Please don't tell Mom," I say.

"Are you okay?"

"Yes. You promise you won't tell Mom?"

"Depends. What are you doing there?"

121

I tell him the story, making it as brief as I can. Everything from how she and the Scoot were friends to the book and how Jaycee wanted to help the Scoot get it to his dad. And how she promised him we would.

"Jesus," he says when I'm done.

"Yeah, I know."

"It's completely moronic, you know that, right?" He laughs though, so I laugh too.

"Yeah," I say. "I know it is."

"Well, good. Then what do you want from me? I mean, are you guys okay?"

"Yeah," I answer. "Well, no. I mean, we're okay, but Jaycee got sick. She threw up and she's pretty hot. Actually, she's burning up. So I'm kind of worried about her."

"What's her temp?"

"I don't know. She's asleep. I don't have a thermometer. I didn't take it."

"Dude, you gotta take it. Aren't there stores around there? If it's too high, you'd better call a doctor. And get her some Tylenol. And make her drink water. Jeez, you're the fever expert. You don't need me to tell you all this."

"Right," I say. "Okay."

"Night, kid," he says.

"Jeremy, if Mom asks, I'm at Ryan's, okay?"

"Yeah, sure. Call me tomorrow."

I hang up. I glance at the clock again. I wonder if the gift shop is still open.

122

When I get down to the lobby, the gift shop lights are out and there's a woman just locking the door. "My sister's sick," I say frantically. "I just need some Tylenol and a thermometer. And some ginger ale if you've got it. Please," I add, "my mom just sent me down." She looks at me oddly, but opens the door and flicks the lights on, points me to the back corner.

"Next to the Band-Aids," she says.

I run and grab the stuff and walk to the glass fridge and call out, "Do you have ginger ale?"

"Below the Sprite," she says.

Eventually I find it there, a large bottle of Schweppes, and pull it from the fridge. To its right are cans of Cherry RC Cola. Just like in the vending machine. And that's when it hits me. The water tower. The cherry cola. And, now, the fever.

I should have seen it coming.

I take the stuff to the register and grab a bag of Ritz crackers and another of cashews and dump the whole mess on the counter where the woman is waiting for me.

"Does your mom want this one?" She picks up the thermometer and waves it at me.

"Yes," I say. "And the Tylenol."

"Okay then. Just making sure." She rings it up and I pay and head back to the room.

Jaycee is still asleep, her breath crazy fast, her hair matted with sweat. I take the glass of now-melted ice to the bathroom, empty it, and pour some ginger ale in, then walk back over to the bed and tap her gently. She doesn't react.

I put my hand on her cheek. Burning hot.

I shake her harder. She doesn't wake up. I sit on the bed beside her and keep shaking her.

"Jaycee, you have to wake up," I say loudly. "Jaycee, wake up!"

She moves a little and pulls the blanket over her head and whimpers. I lean into her. "Jaycee, you have to let me take your temp. You have to drink something. You have to take some Tylenol." I shake her until she opens her eyes. She looks at me confused. "You have to drink something," I say. "Please. Sit up for a second. You gotta trust me. I'm the Fever King. You'll be okay. But you gotta drink something."

She pushes herself up. Her eyes are so red and glassy. "What time is it?" she asks.

"Almost seven. Come on, take a sip. And we should probably take your temperature." I hold out two Tylenol and the thermometer. "Come on," I say. "Then you can go back to sleep."

She looks at the stuff in my hand, and then me. And then she starts to laugh. But she's crying too, so it comes out all mixed up. Laughing and crying at the same time. She's delirious. I know this well. I know how a high fever can make a person delirious.

"What?" I ask. "What's so funny?"

"The thermometer," she says, but she's babbling so it's hard to tell what she means.

"Here it is." I try to hand it to her, but she hangs there limply and laugh-cries some more. Finally she lifts her head and musters the energy to talk.

"It's a rectal, Nick."

"What?"

"The little stubby tip. It goes in a baby's butt." She shakes her head, then presses her hand against her forehead like the effort hurts her. "Oh God," she says, "my head is killing me."

I turn the thermometer and look at it. It does have a stubby tip. No wonder the gift shop lady asked me if I wanted this one.

"So you can't use it then?" She tries to laugh her big busting-out Jaycee laugh, but it only comes out like a whimper.

"I'm sick, Nick. I'm really, really sick."

"I know you are," I say. "It'll be okay. I always get like this." I push her hair off her forehead. It's soaking wet.

"But I never do. I never get this way."

"It was the water tower," I tell her. "I saw it when we got here. And then the cherry cola, remember? I should have known." I hold the ginger ale toward her, and, gratefully, she drinks some. I hand the Tylenol to her too.

"What are you talking about?" she asks.

"The water tower, the cherry cola, and now there's a fever. It's some weird trifecta of foreshadowing. You know, like you taught me about in the book? I mean, that's what started the whole bad chain of events at home—my dad leaving and Scooter dying—and now it's happening again."

"No it's not. That's stupid, Nick." She puts the Tylenol on her tongue and swallows them down. "I'll be fine. I've just got some bug." She motions for the thermometer. "Come on, gimme."

"But it's rectal," I say.

"I know. But it's new. Untouched by human hand. Or anus. Just give it to me. I'll do it under my arm."

It takes me a minute to get it out of its case, then she puts it under her arm and we wait for a bit, and then I take it back from her. I twist it away from her in the light to read the mercury. I don't say anything.

"What?" she asks. "Is it bad?"

"Not too bad. But if you want, we could call your mom."

"No!" she says. I look at the readout again. The silver line nearly touches 105 degrees. Her teeth chatter and she pulls her hood up over her head. "Don't you dare, Nick," she pleads.

"Okay. Never mind. Go back to sleep. Don't worry. I'll take care of you."

I sit on the bed next to her and she leans her head on my shoulder. My sleeve dampens where it's resting.

"Thanks," she says.

"No problem. Have another sip though. I'm not kidding. You have to keep drinking. A lot."

"Promise." She takes a few sips.

"Now, go back to sleep," I say. She slips under the blankets and shakes. "Okay, good night. I'm sure you'll be better in the morning."

"I hope so." She rolls onto her side and curls up in a ball like a baby. I rest my hand on her back for a second, then stand up and head toward my room. "Nick," she calls.

"Yeah?"

"Will you stay with me?"

I stare through the door at my made-up bed, at my backpack with no pajamas, at my bags of unopened crackers and nuts and my Rice Krispies treat in a little cluster on the bedspread. I'm not even hungry at all.

"Yeah. Of course," I say.

14

At 6:30 a.m. I awaken, groggy and confused about where I am. It had taken hours to finally fall asleep, and even when I did, I slept fitfully, on top of the covers with all my clothes on. I glance sideways to Jaycee. She's curled up in a blanketed lump. I reach over and tap her. She doesn't stir. I feel the heat circulating.

I contemplate calling Jeremy again, or maybe getting her to a hospital. But deep inside, I know that these things pass and that, as long as I get liquid in her, she'll probably be okay. At least I tell myself this. *Jaycee will be okay.*

I force myself up, to the bathroom, then wander down the hall to get some fresh ice. When I get back, I realize I don't want to bang the ice to bits in the room, so I drag the iron back down the hallway to the ice machine closet and bang it up in there. When I return, I hang the DO NOT DISTURB sign on her door, then rouse her and place a few chips to her lips.

They are dry and cracked from the fever. The chips melt on contact and slip down her chin. I pat it with my sleeve.

She falls back asleep. I lie there and listen to her breathe. At one point she moans, and I wonder seriously whether I should call her mom.

"No, don't!" she whimpers.

"Shhh. Just sleep, crazy girl."

Suddenly she bolts up, and looks at me with big eyes. "We have to find Scooter's dad." I can tell she's only half-conscious, that her thoughts are jumbled with a feverish delirium. It's something I happen to know well. "No, don't," she says again.

"It's okay." I pat her arm and steer her back down. "I won't, Jaycee. Just relax."

"But, we have to find the Scoot's dad," she mumbles again, as if this is even still a possibility.

As if it ever was.

She falls back to sleep.

I pace the room trying to come up with something useful, some sort of idea or plan. Then I think about what Jaycee said the book, or the mouse poem, said about how useless plans can be. I lie down and close my eyes, but as I do Jaycee jumps up, walks to her sneakers, and starts to put them on.

"Hey, where are you going?"

She looks past me with ghost eyes. I know the look. It's the look that will lead you to a water tower.

"I'm going to find him," she says. "Before Scooter dies."

It kills me. It makes me want to cry.

"It's not time yet, Jaycee." I put a firm hand on her shoulder, guide her back to the bed, and pull her sneakers off. "It's barely morning. I promise. I'll wake you when it's time."

I manage to get her to lie down, to settle and go back to sleep.

I turn on the TV and mute it again, and watch the Sesame Street Muppets dance around some letters. Funny how, no matter how old you get, you can still remember their names. Cookie Monster. Elmo. Gordon.

Periodically, Jaycee mumbles gibberish from her sleep— something about clouds and airplanes, or, maybe, olives, then something about a golden retriever. A few more times she says Scooter's name, then, "Dad says so. Yes, I'm telling you, he says so." I watch back and forth between the Muppets and Jaycee, waiting and praying for the fever to burn off the delirium.

By 8:00 a.m. Jaycee has cooled down slightly and is sleeping soundly, and I'm so tired I can barely breathe. But I can't fall back to sleep either, probably because I'm worried.

I go to my room and pull *Of Mice and Men* from my backpack. There's still a Post-it in it from the bus. I walk back to Jaycee's room and lie on the bed and open to that page.

There they are: Lennie in the barn, and Curly's wife in her bright red dress sitting beside him in the straw. Jaycee has drawn an arrow on the bookmark to the spot where she left off with a note that says "Read Here." As if she knew I'd come back to it without her.

" 'If George sees me talkin' to you he'll give me hell,' Lennie said cautiously. 'He tol' me so.' "

The words sound familiar, yet all of it—the bus, Jaycee reading aloud—seems like days ago. Like a hundred hours have gone by. Can it be less than twenty-four hours since we stepped off the bus in Rochester and stood in the parking lot with the GPS in hand?

I settle myself down on a pillow, hold the book above my head and read:

"Her face grew angry. 'Wha's the matter with me?' she cried. 'Ain't I got a right to talk to nobody? Whatta they think I am, anyways? You're a nice guy. I don't know why I can't talk to you. I ain't doin' no harm to you.'

" 'Well, George says you'll get us in a mess.' " I look at Jaycee sleeping and shake my head. Talk about messes.

I close the book and rest it on my stomach. The truth is I'm too tired to read and it's so much better when she reads aloud to me.

I pick the book up again and stare at its cover. The men in the hats, the boring orange road. At least now I know which man is Lennie and which is George. I turn it over and read the little blurb about the author, then flip it open to the title page. And there it is, John Steinbeck's signature. It is kind of cool to see it, knowing how much money it's worth. Above his autograph is a short inscription,

True valor comes in all shapes and sizes—and often
from those you'd least expect.

My throat catches. Maybe that's why Scooter's dad left the book for him.

I lay it back on the bed, then close my eyes and fight tears, which it seems I've had to do a lot lately. I try to think of something else besides the Scoot, and my mind goes to Dad. I try to imagine him so much thinner now. Mom says that he told her his sweats were falling down. He's walked nearly two hundred miles. I wonder what finally made him want to do it, and gave him the courage to try. I also wonder if he's really coming home, or if Jeremy knows things I don't.

I mean, one thing Jeremy's right about is that Mom and Dad haven't seemed too happy in a long time. They argue constantly about stuff that makes me feel bad, like money and Dad's weight. Or about how tired she is because she does all the work while he just lies around. Or about how maybe she wouldn't have to if she hadn't talked him into leaving Manhattan, since she *knew* how much he loved it there, and that New York City is where all the good journalism is. And about how our little hick town has never really felt like home to him.

"I didn't talk you into anything," I heard Mom saying one

night. "We *agreed* Glenbrook was better for a family. That is so very unfair of you."

And Dad yelling back, "We didn't agree. You never asked me. You only heard what you wanted to hear."

I pick up the book again and try to read a few more paragraphs to block out the unhappy thoughts, but suddenly I'm feeling crappy myself, and so damned tired I finally can't keep my eyes from closing.

When I awaken, the room is gray and quiet and Jaycee is gone from the bed. For a split second, I think I've dreamed everything: the Scoot dying, Rochester, the fever.

I sit up, blink, and try to focus.

The shower is running.

I search groggily for the time. The clock on the nightstand reads 3:00 p.m. I've been sleeping for like five hours.

I push myself up out of my stupor, walk to my room, and sit on the bed there and try to regroup. The message light on my cell phone is flashing. I scan through them.

Jeremy, from 11 a.m.: *"R u ok, kid?"*

Jeremy, from 1:15 p.m.: *"Nick, text me. All ok?"*

Jeremy, from 2:25 p.m.: *"Dude, seriously, in an hr I call the Troops."*

Crap.

I text back, *"Yes, all ok, fell asleep, sorry,"* and drop the phone back on the bed.

I go to the bathroom and brush my teeth. In the mirror, I look like death warmed over. I run my hands under water and push them through my hair, and emerge as the shower turns off in the next room. A minute later, I hear the sound of her bathroom door opening. I walk quietly over to the door between our rooms and pull it shut, then sit on my bed.

I'm suddenly starving. I open my bag of cashews and pop in a few, but they taste lousy because of my minty-fresh breath. I pick up my phone and text Jeremy again:

"Hey."

"Wat up?" he texts back within seconds.

"Just checkg in. J is better. Wat r u doing?"

"Jerking off to heart's content—all alone in house."

I laugh. *"Dude,"* I text back, *"TMI."*

"No prob," he answers. *"Btw, glad all OK."*

I stare at the phone and smile. I wish I could be like Jeremy, so comfortable with all that sex stuff. With his body and girls and all that. Even joking about it makes me squeamish and uncomfortable. Like the whole thing with kissing Jaycee. Just thinking about it makes my palms sweat and my ears burn, because how will I know what I'm doing? Jeremy says I shouldn't worry. That when it's time, it all comes naturally. But seriously, I think it's *more than* time.

Then again, she's been sick and puking for hours, so what is my mind doing there?

I throw my cell back on the bed, fish a clean T-shirt, underwear, and socks out of my backpack, and head to the bathroom to shower.

The shower is strong and good. Like the kind you can't get at home anymore because it uses too much water. I shampoo and soap myself, then turn my face to the stream. The hot water is just what I need. I want to stay in here for hours, letting the warmth fall over me, but I should get out and check on Jaycee. I towel off and put on my clean stuff plus my one pair of slept-in jeans, and leave the bathroom to check on her.

She startles me, because I'm still drying my hair with the towel and when I look up, there she is, sitting right on my bed. She's dressed in her cargos and orange sneakers, same sweatshirt, hood pulled up over her head. She looks almost normal again.

"Oh, hey!" I say. "I didn't expect you in here. Good thing I got dressed in there." I motion behind me to the bathroom.

"Yeah, good thing." She rolls her eyes. "You know, I've seen tighty whities before."

"Boxer briefs," I say, trying not to blush. "So you're feeling better?"

"A little," she says, then, "and you got this while you were showering."

She tosses my cell phone to me. There's another message from Jeremy.

135

"So, now that she's better, you gonna bag her, bro? ;)"

Crap.

"My brother's a jerk," I say. My face burns bright red. "He's just joking around."

"I know," she says, but I still feel awful. I don't want her to think I'm that kind of guy. I blurt out, "Jaycee, I swear, I've barely even kissed a girl." And, of course, the "barely even" is a lie.

"I know that too." She laughs. "No biggie, Nick, really. So now what?"

"Um . . ."

"Not about *that*. I'm talking about Scooter. About finding his dad. We seriously only have like two days left."

"Yeah. Best laid plans," I say.

She raises her eyebrows, then smiles. But it's not her usual "Ha-ha-you're-an-idiot" smile. There's something more to it this time, like she's genuinely impressed that I made the reference, but something else too.

"What?" I ask. "Don't look at me like that. I listen. I pay attention. I'm not just some dopey jerk, Jaycee. It's not like I don't care." She stares at me, her amazing husky-dog eyes looking right into me. And then I know what the look is. It's grateful. The girl is grateful. "Come on, sicko." I hold my hand out to her. She looks at me and sighs, then gets up, puts her hand in mine, and, just like that—that simple—we're holding hands. "Let's go. We'll go downstairs, get something to

136

eat. Crackers or something light. And then we can see how you feel."

We head down and through the lobby and into the brisk Rochester air. It's the twenty-eighth of October, nearly four o'clock. Already a dusky gray out. This time of year always makes me melancholy. I hate when it's dark before we're barely even home from school.

As we walk, I feel groggy, like I've been in an endless tunnel or something. Or at least a long, dark hall. But outside I start to feel like me again, like life is a little more normal. Well, as normal as it can be with Jaycee walking next to me in Rochester. I look at her and she shivers a little, so I put my arm around her.

We return to our deli and get ourselves something to eat. Since yesterday, the deli has gone full-out on the Halloween decorations. I had forgotten about the holiday altogether. Orange and black streamers and paper ghosts hang everywhere, and a life-size cardboard witch stands in the corner. There's a candy bowl at the cash register with a white rubber hand. The kind that reaches out and snatches when you go for it.

And for some reason, I remember the year Scooter and I were around eight or nine, and he dressed up as Yoda for Halloween. Everyone kept mistaking him for E.T. At first it pissed him off, but then we started joking and trying to come up with things to say that combined the two, E.T. and Yoda, like "Phone home, at nine hundred years you will," until both of us were peeing in our pants.

I must be smiling, because Jaycee says, "What?"

"Nothing. Just all the Halloween stuff. It made me think of something."

"I miss him too," she says.

When it's our turn to order, I choose a ham and Swiss cheese with lettuce, tomato, mayo, and bacon on a twelve-inch sub and Jaycee gets Saltines and ginger ale.

"Are you sure that's enough?" I ask. She nods and says, "Better not push things too much."

There's a small park down the block, so we go and sit there and eat. By the time we're done, Jaycee looks like crap again, and besides, she's shivering nonstop.

"Come on, Jaycee. Let's go back to the room. It's dark anyway. We'll start fresh tomorrow. We'll rent a movie or something."

She doesn't argue, which really tells you something.

Which is why it's no surprise that, by the time we get back to the room, she's puking up her crackers, and her temp is back up to 102 degrees. I'm not as worried now though, because she's been up and around, and it's not nearly as bad as it was earlier. And I'm a fever expert, so I know how the whole cycle goes. She'll maybe spike again tonight, but she'll be much better by morning. Until then, you've just got to let it run its course.

I get her fresh ice and tuck her in, then sit on the edge of her bed with the Steinbeck book.

"Go to sleep. I'll watch a movie. Or read this thing, maybe." I wave the book at her. "Because I'm sure something hugely fun is about to happen in here since this story is chockfull of happy surprises." I laugh at my sarcasm and settle myself in on my side on top of the bedspread, assuming she'll want me to stay again.

Jaycee swats backward at me through the tangled mess of her sweatshirt sleeves and blankets and says, "Shut up, Gardner. And, yeah, please don't go away."

The swat isn't forceful, but it's comforting, because it seems more like the good old, less-sick Jaycee.

"Ouch," I say. "Must you?"

"I must, Lennie," she says.

15

The next morning we both sleep late, and then Jaycee, who is much better but also starving, insists on ordering room service, her treat.

Pancakes in me, and oatmeal *and* waffles in her, we're finally out in the sunshine by 11:00 a.m. It's Saturday morning, the twenty-ninth of October, but you might as well tell me it's December. Or July. It's like I've lost all track of time, and of my real life, and all there is now is Rochester, Jaycee, and me.

It's as if we've slipped into a vortex and arrived in this town, and yet it's the only place I remember, the only place I've ever known. Half the time, I barely think of Mom, or Dad, or even Jeremy for that matter.

I know we're here for a reason—to find Scooter's dad—but the truth is that that reason doesn't really matter so much to me. Or maybe the real truth is it never did. At least not once Scooter died. It's not that I don't care about helping the Scoot because of course I do. I loved the guy. I guess I just can't see how finding his father now will make any difference to him. Plus, in my heart, I think the book should stay with MaeLynn.

Of course, I don't say any of this to Jaycee. It matters a lot to her. So I want to find Guy Reyland and deliver the book for her sake as much as I always did.

Jaycee whistles as we walk, the GPS chiming in periodically from her pocket. She's her bouncy old self again. As if the fever never happened. I mean, I'm used to it. Fevers are just like that sometimes. At any rate, I'm happy to be walking and talking and laughing again, even if we're back on our crazy mission.

I try to keep the pace slow, not wanting to push her too much, but once she's set her mind to something she's in fast motion; you really can't hold her back. She's three steps ahead of me most of the time.

We've decided to head downtown to the newsroom, the NBC affiliate in Rochester. Jaycee says newsmen know everyone and everything, so we'll see if they know him there.

"Where better than a newsroom," she asks, "to find a missing person?"

"A police station?" I suggest. "The county jail? The gutter? A graveyard? Especially if the missing guy is a scumbag."

She punches me. "You're such an upbeat companion. And, yes, maybe we should try all those too."

"Speaking of upbeat," I say, "I finished that dumb book of yours."

"You did?" She slows down and grabs my arm. "Why didn't you tell me? Isn't it just brutal?"

I laugh. "Yeah, Jaycee, it's brutal. So, um, thanks for that. Because there's nothing better than reading a really sad book when one of your best friends is burning up with a fever and the other one has just died."

She turns and looks at me. But I know what I've said, and I mean it. And I'm glad that she knows.

"Sorry, I guess it is sad," she says, still holding on to my sweatshirt sleeve but picking up our pace again. "But beautiful too, right? How all they've got is each other?"

"I guess," I say. "It just seemed sad to me, period. Plus, I don't know how he could do what he did."

"He needed to," she says. "It was the ultimate act of friendship." She drops my arm and grabs my hand instead, lacing her fingers through mine.

"I guess," I say again, because now that she's holding my hand I'm having a hard time concentrating.

"I just like how the book shows how plans go wrong," she says. "I mean, their dream was to buy a ranch and for Lennie to tend to the rabbits. But you know from the outset there's going to be a problem, that something will get messed up. Like the Burns poem says, you know, 'The best laid plans of mice and men go oft awry.' "

"Yeah," I say. "I totally get it now. Really. Best laid plans of mice and men. From the book's title." She rolls her eyes like she doesn't believe me, but I'm not kidding. I do understand it. At least, I feel like I do.

"Yes. From the title. But of course the title comes from the English translation. The original Robert Burns poem is Scottish. So the poem doesn't say 'plans' it says 'schemes.' And it doesn't say 'go oft awry,' it says 'gang aft agley.' But trust me, you'll learn all this soon enough."

"Aft gang agley?"

"Yeah. Well, the other way around. *Gang aft* agley. I think that's Scottish for 'go often awry.' The real line is 'The best laid schemes o' mice an' men gang aft agley.'"

"The o' is a nice touch," I say.

"Anyway, the bottom line is that George would have done anything to help Lennie. He wanted to do right by him." She squeezes my hand tighter.

We walk the next few blocks quietly, listening to the GPS speak its robotic commands from inside her sweatshirt pocket: "*Turn left on East Main, go point three miles, turn right at East Avenue, go point seven miles . . .*" As we walk, I glance at her, wishing I could know what she's thinking. Occasionally, she turns and smiles at me. When we finally reach the NBC building, we pause at the double revolving doors.

It looks mostly like a regular old office building, not nearly as exciting as the one in New York City with its block-long picture windows and giant photos of Matt Lauer and Al Roker in the lobby. I let go of Jaycee and wipe my hand on my jeans. I can't believe how sweaty it is. What a dork I am.

"Okay," she says, "cross your fingers something turns up here." She spins the door and pushes me in, then slips into the quickly narrowing opening along with me.

"What will you say if it does?"

"I don't know." She shrugs. "I'll figure something out. I was off my game Thursday. Too sick. But today I'll be brilliant. Something will come to me. You know it always does."

I nod in hopeful agreement, especially since, as we emerge into the large lobby, there's a big, bald security guard who looks like a WWE wrestler headed in our direction. "Now's your chance," I say.

"Hey, Jim," Jaycee says instantly, waving and smiling as he approaches. I'm stunned. *She knows him.* She flashes him a great big grin. "Goin' up to the newsroom again." He looks at her funny, like he's not sure. "J.P.'s stepdaughter," she says. "You remember. J.P. Amato? News 10, Albany. He's doing work up there." She turns her head a little toward the far wall. "He's there with Phil Brenner, my uncle. They're both expecting us, me and my brother, Nick." She shoves me forward.

I have no idea what or who she's talking about—other than J.P., of course—but the guard obviously does. He takes a big step backward, says, "Of course, Ms. Amato," and ushers us in and points us toward the elevators.

"Second floor," he calls, nodding.

"I know," she yells back, waving.

"Okay, redeemed," I say, marveling. "So, you know him?"

"Never saw him before in my life."

"But you called him by his . . ."

"Name tag." She pokes my chest where a tag would be pinned. I laugh, impressed. "You are such a noob," she says.

"But still, he clearly knows J.P.? I mean, he didn't argue or anything."

She shrugs. "Who knows? You say it with authority, and they believe you. And they don't want to get in trouble. TV people can be pretty obnoxious and haughty. I should know." I laugh. "Or maybe he does," she adds. "Maybe he's heard his name tossed around. Like I said, he comes up here sometimes. For a story or something. A lot of people know J.P. I told you, the name does come with perks."

We reach the elevator bank and Jaycee pushes the up button.

"Well, what about Phil Brenner?" I ask. "He's not your uncle then?"

She turns my body around and nods. Staring from across the lobby is a huge framed poster of a man with glasses and a mustache, in a suit and tie, with a blond woman in a red dress. Across the top, it says *Spend Your Mornings with Phil & Amy*, and on the bottom, *Phil Brenner & Amy Reed, The Phil & Amy Show, Weekdays at 10:00 a.m.*

The girl is good.

When we reach the second floor, it's not hard to find

the newsroom. It takes up the whole entire place. Even on a Saturday, the place buzzes with activity. There's a large double steel door to our left, and the rest of the wall is an enormous window, all glass, so you can see in. Above the window is an unlit ON-AIR sign, its red words not yet glowing.

The studio looks pretty much like what you'd expect: a green screen, a wood platform with an interview area that looks a little like a living room with a small round table and two chairs set up in front of a dark navy curtain, a bunch of cameras, and a large gray news desk where a male and female anchor sit, already in their places. They're talking to each other, but you can tell it's just horsing around, while the cameramen work to set up around them. Jaycee says, "Come on. Let's see who we can talk to. It should only take a few minutes."

She walks in like it's nothing through the heavy steel doors. I hang back a few steps and watch her as she saunters up to one of the cameramen.

"We're looking for a missing person," she says. "My stepdad, J.P. Amato, News 10, Albany, he's doing a feature on him." She unzips the side pocket of her backpack and pulls something out. It's a key chain with a tag on it. She holds it out to him, then hands it to me. It's a laminated press pass with her photo on it, for News 10, Albany. She flashes a smile at me. "He's following up a lead at the courthouse, so I'm helping out here today." I think it's pretty smooth, but the guy still questions her.

146

"You're a little young to be helping out on your own, no?" He bends down to adjust something on the camera.

"Not on my own." She tugs on my sleeve. "My brother is with me."

The guy glances up at me from where he's kneeling. "Well, who you looking for, someone who works around here?"

"Not sure," Jaycee says. "The guy is missing. Figured someone here might know the name. Guy Reyland."

"Reyland?" he repeats.

"Yeah, Guy Reyland."

He shakes his head. "Never heard of him. Maybe you want to try the police station. Or City Hall."

"We will. Next on the list." She gives me a look. "But since my stepdad's part of the News 10 team, we figured we'd snoop around here first."

"Sorry, wish I could help you," he says. "Try Linda and Mike. Maybe they've heard of him." He points to the news desk. "Trust me, Linda pretty much knows everyone."

"Thanks," Jaycee says. "Will do."

We walk over to the news desk, my eyes glued on Jaycee. It's amazing to me how fearless she is; the old Jaycee is back, with all the confidence in the world.

"Hey," she says when we reach the desk, then repeats her whole stupid story to the newscasters. The man is making notes on some blue index cards, barely looks up, just shrugs. Like he's way too busy to even think about it.

"Guy Reyland," I blurt out, because I want to contribute. "We really need to find him." Jaycee shoots me a look like I shouldn't have.

"For our stepdad," she says, "for a story."

Linda, a youngish-looking woman with short dark hair and one of those moles near her lip, scratches her head. "Reyland you said, right? Hold on a sec."

She taps across the newsroom floor in her high heels and green suit, to an old, metal file cabinet against the side wall. She opens and closes drawers, pulling folders out and stuffing them back in. Jaycee elbows me and gives me a look like "I told you so," and I raise my eyebrows hopefully. Finally she heads back, holding a folded newspaper section in her hand.

"Funny," she says, waving it, "I thought I remembered the name. Cute place too. I've been there a few times. But not lately. And of course this is from years ago, so who knows? Anyway, hope it helps you kids. Now, we're about to go on air, so you have to clear out of here."

"Can we take this?" Jaycee asks.

"Sure, I doubt we need it anymore." Jaycee thanks her, and we head back out toward the elevators.

"Open it!" I say, reaching over as soon as we're in the hall.

"Chill." She hugs it to her chest and pushes the button. The doors open right away. Nobody but us. We step in and they close again, slowly. "Okay," she finally says.

She unfolds the paper and holds it in front of us. It's the

148

Lifestyles section of the Rochester *Times Union*. June 2004. There's a photo of a decent-looking guy with long dark hair, squinting in front of a large restaurant window. It's just a photo with a caption under it, no article or anything to go with it. The caption says, "Local poet Guy R. Reyland opens Front Street burger joint / luncheonette. Says Reyland of his new venture, 'Let's hope burgers pay better than words.' "

"It's him, right?" I say, touching my finger to the photo. Of course I don't really recognize him, and there's no resemblance to the Scoot. Then again, there wouldn't be. But his name is right there: *Guy Reyland*. I mean, how many Guy Reylands can there be? It's definitely him.

"It's gotta be," Jaycee says. "Did you see it?"

"The caption? Yeah. The dude writes poems. I mean, that's totally weird."

"No," she says, moving my fingers away. "The name of the luncheonette."

16

The GPS leads us to Broadway and Front Street. The whole way, Jaycee chatters excitedly.

"Remember that corporation on Front Street? That was him. That must have been him and we didn't know it." I nod and try to keep up with her. "Plus it makes perfect sense that he's a poet, you know. They're all crazy, flaky, schizos and alcoholics who can't hold a job or keep a family." She turns around, jogs backward, facing me. "Edgar Allen Poe, Sylvia Plath," she says to prove her point. "You name it, Nick, you think poet, you think weird loner who kills himself or disappears." She flashes a huge smile at me. The girl is clearly revved up.

"What about Dr. Seuss?" I ask, and she rolls her eyes, which makes me laugh.

As we finally turn onto Front Street, our British guide chimes from Jaycee's pocket: *Two-tenths of a mile, you have reached your destination.*" In another minute we're standing in front of it, my heart pounding a little, both our mouths open. Across the plate glass window it reads *Scooter's Olde Fashioned Luncheonette.* To tell you the truth, it makes me want to cry.

"Scooter would have loved that," Jaycee says.

Judging from the huge crowd packed just inside the door, lots of people love it.

"I guess lunchtime on a Saturday wasn't the best time to come," she says, thinking what I'm thinking. It's almost two, but it's still a zoo in there.

"Do you think he just owns it or works here?"

She shrugs, and I don't have an answer either. I hadn't really thought about it until now. I had just pictured him flipping burgers in the back when I saw the photo. But the caption said he owned it, not cooked there. I mean, he may not even be inside. Unless he lives at the place. I turn and look at her. We're face-to-face, my hand squeezed in hers. I realize she's been holding it the whole time.

I suddenly, overwhelmingly, want to kiss her.

I try to clear my head.

"I don't know. What do you think?" is all I manage, which is dumb because I'm stupidly repeating my own question.

"I don't know either." She squeezes my hand harder. "Maybe we should sit down and order something. Have some lunch and wait for the place to quiet down? Then see if we can find him or ask for the manager or something."

"Okay," I say. "I guess we need to put our names down and wait?"

She nods, then pushes me ahead of her. "Go to it, Lennie," she says.

I leave Jaycee standing just inside the door and make my way through the crowd in the vestibule and leave my name with the maître d', then squeeze back through to Jaycee.

"No Guy?" she asks when I reach her.

"No Guy. And at least fifteen minutes for a table."

In the vestibule, the benches are all taken. We have to stand, and I'm squished right up against her. Our sweatshirts touch and her face is right in front of mine. Her eyes are amazing, and her lips look really soft. I try not to think about how bad I want to kiss them. I mean, here we are, finally about to find Scooter's dad, so I shouldn't be thinking about that.

The crowd shifts and loosens a little as a table for four is called. I watch them as they're herded to their table, but Jaycee pulls my face back to hers. Our noses nearly touch. I can feel her warm breath on my chin. For a second, I'm sure she's going to kiss me and I can just stop worrying about it all.

But she doesn't. She tugs on the strings to my hood. "Thanks, Nick. Thanks for coming with me."

"No prob," I say, and she laughs, and I'm pretty sure she's laughing at me. But I don't mind so much because there's something sweet about it too.

"I'm serious," she says. "I know you think I'm crazy. I know

152

you don't care if we find Scooter's dad. That you didn't even think that we should. Seriously, I know that. I know that you did this completely for me." She looks straight in my eyes.

I'm not sure what to say or do. I mean, there are a whole bunch of strangers around us. I nod and reach my arm out and somehow manage to place it around her, on her back, and then move it a little, in a lame sort of combined pat and hug. She smiles and pulls my other arm around her too. It's hard to leave them there now. I feel self-conscious, but I manage to anyway.

"It's just that everything's always so broken, you know, Nick? People leave. People die. New, stupider people come. People are there and then gone. And you just have to sit there and take it. Deal with it. Accept it for what it is. But maybe once in a while you get a chance to fix it. At least a little. Or at least try. Or pretend that you can. Sometimes you just want to know that you tried."

"There is no try, remember?" But I hug her tighter because I can tell she needs it, plus maybe I'm starting to get the hang of this holding and hugging thing. "I know what you're saying though," I add.

"I have to pee," she says, which isn't exactly what I'm expecting now that I'm feeling all suave. But then why would I expect anything else with Jaycee?

"Okay." I let go and shove my hands into my pockets. A couple ahead of us are called. "Hurry back," I say.

Jaycee bobs off to the maître d's desk, then into the center of the restaurant. I watch her, and then just the tip of her green hood, disappear and reappear until I finally can't see it anymore. Then, for the first time since we walked in, I look around.

The vestibule wall is crowded with photos. There are shots of people in the restaurant, eating burgers and ice cream sundaes. There are a few headshots of people I don't recognize, but they're autographed so I guess they must be famous, at least by Rochester standards. There's also a framed copy of the newspaper photo. I walk up to it to study it more closely, wondering if maybe I'll also find a photo of MaeLynn or Scooter even, as a baby. Then again he wasn't exactly your magazine-model type of kid.

I turn around to scope out the other walls, and my heart sinks. Opposite where I stand, there's a large, framed, retro-style poster, like from the 1950s or something. It's got a light blue background with a drawing of a huge brown, chocolate sandwich cookie with a graham cracker crust and marshmallow cream oozing out of it. Below that it says *Burry's Scooter Pies. Mmm. Delicious.*

Scooter Pies!

Man, what if that's it? What if that's why the restaurant is called Scooter's Luncheonette, and the Scoot has nothing to do with it? What if Guy Reyland is nothing more than a jerk and a bastard, who didn't even care enough to name a stupid old burger joint after his kid, just like I thought he was?

154

I mean, he clearly didn't care enough about his kid to stay with him, so why would he name a restaurant after him? God, what if his diner's just named after an old-fashioned moon pie cookie, and none of it has anything to do with the Scoot? What will I tell Jaycee?

I scan for her, and catch her hood and then her pigtails bobbing back toward me. I take a deep breath and try to think more clearly. Maybe I should just block the poster. Or maybe I need to tell her. Maybe she needs to know while there's still time to change our minds and go. Because maybe I'm right after all. Maybe the dude doesn't deserve to have a fifteen-thousand-dollar book. Maybe he's a total nobody and a loser who was better off not being found.

But then, Jaycee was so excited to find him, so hopeful that when she did, he'd have a decent bone in his body. If he named the dumb diner after Scooter Pies she'll be crushed.

As she gets closer, I notice she has this weird expression on her face, which makes me wonder if she already knows. Maybe she's seen the same thing. Maybe outside the bathroom there was another poster. Maybe there are posters for Scooter Pies plastered all over the whole damned restaurant.

By the time she gets to me, she's pale and trembling. Maybe it's something else. Maybe she's been sick again.

"Jaycee, are you okay?"

"Yeah, Nick." She nods and clutches my arm. "I am. I'm okay. But you're not. You'd better come with me!"

155

17

She pulls me through the dining area full of people and tables and booths, steers me left and then back, then nudges me into a corner behind a coatrack loaded down with jackets and sweaters. She puts her hands on my shoulders and turns me slowly around.

"Over there, in the far corner," she whispers, "by the tall plant." She takes my chin and directs my head just a little. "That's him, right? I thought I recognized him from the photos."

It takes me a minute to focus my eyes through everything and adjust to his face, so much thinner.

But, yeah, anyway, sitting there is my dad.

You know, Fat Man 2. Who's supposed to be working in New York City.

Also, he's not alone.

Even though I only see the back of her head—her long blond beautiful hair—I know exactly who it is.

"MaeLynn," Jaycee says. She sees it too. She already knew. She's still got hold of my arm. Her fingers dig into me.

And even from here, across the whole stupid room, from behind a mess of coats and sweaters, I can tell everything. Or at least way more than I want to. From the way my dad holds her hands and stares at her with wide googly eyes like some dumb, love struck kid. And from the way she leans in and tilts her head, like some ridiculous crush. One thing is clear. My dad and MaeLynn: no way they're just friends.

You can tell he's madly in love with her.

"They're together, right?" Jaycee finally asks, although it's really more of a statement than a question. I shake my head and shush her. It's obvious. It's obvious that my dad is here with MaeLynn.

There are a million crazy thoughts spinning through my head and buckets and buckets of rage. So much stuff that I can't even move. I stand frozen, watching them. How can he be here? And why is he here with MaeLynn? And how can my dad look so good? So normal and happy and okay? His whole face has thinned, and his neck and upper body, so that he looks much younger. But it's way more than that. It's the way he sits there and smiles.

I fight the tears that want to come.

"Maybe it's just a coincidence?" Jaycee whispers. "There must be a good reason they're here."

I shake my head. "Maybe there's a good reason *she* is," I say, "but why him? What would *he* be doing here?"

"Maybe she came for the same reason we did?" Jaycee says. "To find Scooter's dad."

"Why would she now when Scooter is dead? And even if she did, that would explain her," I say, "but it doesn't explain my father." I squeeze my eyes shut for a second to think, or maybe to keep from crying.

We stand there staring for another minute as Dad eats and talks and rubs his hands up and down MaeLynn's arm, oblivious to us standing just a few tables away. Try as I might, I just can't believe it. I mean, forget everything else for a minute, how is she, *MaeLynn*, sitting there talking and eating and smiling, like everything is normal and okay, when it's only a week since the Scoot died?

"She must need to, Nick," Jaycee says softly, then gives me a look like, *Why are you always so surprised?* "Take it from me. It's just something I know. There's only so much you can cry. Anyway," she whispers, "people are staring at us. We can't stay behind these coats forever." She elbows me and nods at two old women who watch us from a nearby table, annoyed expressions on their faces. "So what do you want to do?"

"I don't know," I say.

"Well, we should do something. We're gonna get yelled at. We're kind of obvious here."

"Yeah, okay," I say. I press hard on my eyes to stop them from tearing up. "I think I just want to go."

"You don't want to talk to him? You don't want to find out what they're doing here?"

"No. We'll find out sooner or later. It's my dad, Jaycee. I think I just need to go."

"Okay." She slides her hand down my arm and slips her fingers into mine. "Whatever you say. Let's just go then."

We start to move out from behind the mess of jackets, but her backpack catches on one and the coatrack tips. I stop it from crashing down, but not before a few jackets fall to the floor.

"Just leave them," I say, but she stoops quickly to pick them up before pulling me toward the door. If they weren't before, I'm sure people are watching us now. But I don't look back, just let her lead me, my legs not feeling like they're even attached to me anymore. When we reach the front door, she finally turns and faces me.

"You okay?" she asks. "You sure you want to leave?" I nod and keep pushing her forward.

"We should have known it, Jaycee," I say after her. "That something crazy would happen. Think about it. When we first got here, there was the water tower, I told you. Then I bought a cherry cola. And then, out of nowhere, you get a fever. What were the chances of that? Then some woman sends us to *Scooter's Luncheonette*! Something bad was bound to happen."

As I say it, tears force their way out, and I know I just

need to get out of here. I can't worry about Scooter or Guy Reyland or anything else that we came for. When the door opens and the sunshine hits me, I feel like I can breathe again. Jaycee feels it too, heaves a sigh of relief and turns to me.

"Best laid plans gone oft awry?" Her eyes search mine with concern.

"Yeah, gangs and gangs of aft gangly."

I mess it up on purpose because it's stupid and I don't care, and I just want to make Jaycee laugh. Because I know if I can just hear her laugh, then maybe I won't really start to bawl. And she does, she laughs, which at this point is what I need most of all. I take her hand and we start to walk down Front Street again, back in the direction of the hotel.

As we walk, I try not to let my mind go to all the crazy places that it wants to go. To Mom and Dad, and to Jeremy saying I told you so, and to the news crew and the stupid follow-up story that is forming in my brain, about how "Fat Man 2 Leaves Family and Marries Dead Kid's Mother." We make it barely half a block before I hear Dad call my name.

"Nick, hold up. Nick! Wait! Come on!"

I don't stop. I don't want to talk to him.

"Nick!" Jaycee yanks my arm hard to stop me. She points. I whip my head around. He jogs toward me, his face already dripping with sweat. "Jesus, kid, stop! Lemme talk to you."

I yank my arm and try to keep going, but Jaycee lunges

and grabs my hood and pulls forcefully this time. She nearly chokes me. "Nick, stop! Just stop!" Her eyes plead. I glare back at her. "At least hear him out," she says.

"For what? I mean, what can he possibly say?" I look back at him. He leans down, hands on knees, breathing hard. Maybe he'll finally have a heart attack and be done with it.

I turn to Jaycee again, hoping for understanding. Instead she says, "You really should hear him out."

"Why?"

"Because he wants you to."

"So?"

"So, at least you *have* your dad."

At that moment something in her eyes is so clear, I want to trust her. And, more important, I want to do right by her. I look from her back to my dad again, who stands there panting like a dog. Coming up behind him is MaeLynn, her face twisted into a mess of concern, like she doesn't know if she should come or go.

Go, I think, *you should definitely go.* Dad I can deal with, but definitely not MaeLynn. *But then, she's Scooter's mom.*

I jam my hands in my pockets and swallow, and take some breaths until I can get myself to feel solid. "Christ, what?" I finally manage.

"What are you doing here, Nick? Does your mother know where you are? For Pete's sake, what are you doing here in Rochester?"

161

What am I doing here? That's what he wants to know? What am I doing!

I glare at him, refuse to answer. I mean, how is this about *me*? Here he is without Mom—and *with* MaeLynn, of all people—acting like an ass, like some thirteen-year-old hormonal idiot, and he's giving *me* the third degree?

"We were trying to find Scooter's dad."

I whip around at Jaycee. I know she's just trying to be helpful, and yet I'm still furious at her for betraying me. She makes her eyes wide and mouths "What did you want me to do?" then shrugs and turns back to them. "We were looking for Mr. Reyland."

MaeLynn stares for a second with her mouth open, then laughs—not in a happy or mean way, more like in disbelief.

"Guy, honey?" she asks in her sweet southern drawl. "Oh dear God, Guy is dead." She looks to Dad, then back at Jaycee again. "He died a few months ago. I needed to take care of Scooter, but now, well, I came up here to straighten out some things." She motions behind her toward the diner, but then realizes this probably means nothing to us, and sighs. "Well, it's complicated," she says. But of course we already know more than she thinks we do.

"Wait, Guy is dead?" Jaycee's voice breaks. Her face is completely fallen. She hasn't gotten past the first sentence.

"Yes, honey, dead. A few months ago. My goodness, why would you kids be looking for him?"

"Dead?" Jaycee says again. She blinks tears away.

"Yes. I'm sorry. He had serious problems. *Serious*. And Scooter had absolutely no relationship with him. Why would you think you should come looking for him?"

Jaycee opens her mouth to say something, but I squeeze her arm. Maybe there are things that Scooter wouldn't want us to tell. Or maybe he wouldn't care. My head is spinning. I can't keep everything straight.

"So why is he here?" I indicate my dad. He's caught his breath some, stands quietly watching MaeLynn.

"He was helping me, Nick. It's a long story. Come on back inside. We'll have some tea and I'll explain things."

I snort, like a huge, sarcastic laugh. Because I don't want tea. Tea is idiotic, and I'm totally pissed again. Because why the hell is my dad here, in Rochester, with MaeLynn? Instead of where he belongs. Home, in Glenbrook. With Mom. Or at least where he's *supposed* to be, in New York City, which, apparently, is also a big, fat lie. I feel the tears come again.

I turn back to Jaycee. "I really need to leave," I say.

"But Scooter . . ." she says, ignoring me and looking at MaeLynn again. "He didn't know that Guy was dead?"

MaeLynn's eyes dart away for a second. "He was dying himself, honey. He never saw the man. There was no point in telling him."

"But . . ." Jaycee says.

"Come on, Jaycee, you're not going to get straight

163

answers. All you'll get is bullshit. A whole bunch of bullshit and lies." I take her arm, then turn back to glare at my dad. "Everything they say is a lie." I start to pull her with me, but she looks at me with those tears in her eyes. "Come on," I try, "we already got what we came for, right? We found Scooter's dad. He's dead. Buried. Gone. Just like we thought. The dude's a ghost, Jaycee."

I start to walk, whether or not Jaycee's coming with me.

"Nick!" my dad still calls, but I ignore him. "I tried to tell you. I sent you a ton of e-mails! Your mother knows."

I cover my ears but it's too late. I can't stop the tears after that.

Jaycee hangs back for a second, but then runs and catches up. She doesn't try to say anything, just walks beside me and clings to my arm.

MaeLynn calls after us. "Nick! Kids, wait up. I forgot! Oh dear! It's important! I forgot something!"

I shake my head. No way I'm stopping. I'm done. I don't want to hear any more. But of course Jaycee yanks on me, tries to get me to wait. I slow a little. We've gained enough distance. MaeLynn runs after us, her purse hanging open. She's waving some stupid envelope in the air.

"I was supposed to give this to you!"

"I don't want it!" I yell, then pick up our pace again. *I don't give a crap.* I really don't care what she has.

I keep going, even with Jaycee hanging behind. She'll come

164

or she won't. She doesn't always get to make up my mind. A few seconds later she's caught up to me again. "Who cares, right?" she says, and slips her hand back in mine.

And then we walk, the two of us. I know my way back. It's easy enough: Broadway to East Avenue to East Main. Then back to our hotel and away from this stupid town. Away from Dad, and MaeLynn, and Scooter's dumb, dead dad. Away from all these endless plans gone awry.

And without realizing it, I'm running. Jogging slowly at first, but then faster and faster. Jaycee's running too. She's running right beside me. And we just keep on running. Just me and Jaycee, the cars whizzing by, the wind on our faces, the tears still coming, till my legs ache and I can't breathe or think anymore.

When we're almost back, I slow down.

And I walk.

And I breathe.

And I think that, as long as she's here with me, maybe it will all somehow be okay.

18

Back in the hotel room, I can't focus on anything.

Jaycee tosses her backpack on my bed and says, "So?"

I toss mine there too.

The door between our rooms is still propped open. Jaycee's side is immaculate. Housekeeping's been in here. I wonder if they noticed that my bed was still made up.

I shrug, go into the bathroom, close the door, take a piss, and drink from the tap. I don't even bother with a glass. I'm too thirsty and too tired. Just stick my whole mouth under and drink. When I'm done, I stand there for a while staring at nothing, then wipe my mouth with a hand towel, toss it on the floor, and walk out.

Jaycee lies on her back, her legs hanging over the bottom of the bed, our backpacks placed on the pillows like severed heads. I lie down next to her and stare at the white spackled ceiling and say nothing. My cell phone buzzes urgently inside my pocket.

I don't need to look at it. I know who the messages are from. Already there are like fifty texts from my dad. They started on the way back to the hotel. He wants me to call him, but I'm not going to. I don't want to hear. Finally, when it buzzes again, I pull it out and look at it. Now there are three from Jeremy. I toss it at Jaycee. It pegs her on the arm.

"Sorry. You kill it," I tell her. "Throw it at the wall or something."

She holds it above her in the air, clicks down through the texts with her thumb, fiddles with the settings or something, then puts it back down on the bed.

"Yeah, you really showed it," I say. "Thanks." She laughs and stares at the ceiling.

"Parents are such idiots," she finally says. "They ought to have to take tests, sign some kind of contract in blood."

I grunt something meaningless back, then roll my head to the side and stare out the window. It's already nearly dark outside. I don't know how that happened. In the distance there are trees and the silhouette of a large construction crane. Beyond that, I think I can make out the water tower. I shake my head.

Jaycee reaches out and drops her hand on my thigh, then leaves it as if it belongs there. I'm grateful for that. We just lie there like this for I don't know how long. I'm really, really tired, so I'm happy not to have to try to talk or think anymore. Honestly, I don't want to think about any of it. But then she rolls over, sits up, and drags a backpack down toward her.

167

I listen as she unzips it, searches around inside, and pulls out the book and fans through it. *Of Mice and Men*, by John Steinbeck. I know it's the book. I can tell. I don't have to turn around and see it.

And I know she wants me to ask her why she's taken it out—that she's trying to get my attention—which, for some reason, all of a sudden annoys me. I just don't want to talk about it. Not about Dad or MaeLynn or the Scoot, or his dead, loser ghost of a dad. I don't want to hear about any of it anymore. Not today. Not in Rochester. Not now. Maybe not as long as I live. But especially not right now. I'm just tired of it all. And I really just want to go home.

She pages through it.

I just want to go home.

"Put it away, Jaycee," I say. "It was a stupid idea anyway. The whole thing. I mean, you do know that, right? Even Jeremy said so." I watch one glob of spackle-within-spackle that looks like a humpback whale with a long beady eye. It stares back at me. Jaycee doesn't answer. "Thinking we could find Scooter's dad," I dig.

"Whatever," she says.

"I mean, even if he *wasn't* dead." It's cold. It's cruel of me.

"A promise is a promise," she says. She shoves the book back in her pack and zips it. And stands. "At least I do what I say I'll do when it comes to my friends. I can live with that."

"Well it was stupid to agree to it. We shouldn't have promised in the first place. Like we agreed. Then it wouldn't have been a problem." I don't know why I'm being so mean, why I'm pushing things. What's done is done. So why am I suddenly so mad at Jaycee? It's not her fault that Scooter died, or that my big, fat, formerly obese dad is in Rochester sneaking around with MaeLynn.

But I am. I can't help it. All of a sudden I'm completely, totally mad at her. Really, really mad. My throat swells with the effort to choke back tears.

"You're a jerk, you know it?" she says. "Yeah, you're right. Your way is better. Best to avoid all problems, Nick. Because, God forbid you have to deal with something, actually stand up and be a man. Best to run and hide. Even if it means deserting your dying friend. So yeah, I'm an idiot. I can live with that. But at least I stick by my friends. At least I'm not afraid to." She shoulders her backpack and turns to walk away. I grab her arm.

"What does that mean?"

"Nothing," she says.

"What does it mean?" My voice cracks. She yanks her arm away, hikes her backpack up, and walks out, letting the door slam behind her.

The air rings with the bang of it, then everything is quiet.

I lie back down and stare at the ceiling.

I don't know for how long.

Once in a while my cell phone buzzes next to me, and I pick it up to make sure it's not Jaycee. It's not. Once it's Dad. A few times, my idiot brother. I don't answer any of them. I just lie there staring and wondering if Jaycee will come back. Or how I'll get home without her. She has the money, after all.

I don't worry about her. She's tougher than I am. She'll be okay. She doesn't need *me*. I need *her*; not the other way around. Even so, I don't worry about me either. It's just weird. It's sort of like I don't care. But maybe like I care so much I can't think about it. I don't know what's wrong with me. I just feel, mostly, completely numb.

So I lie there and stare at the whale who stares back at me, his big eye all lonely and sad. Until I stare long enough and the ceiling starts to waffle and blur, and the whale morphs and disappears. I mean, it's still there somewhere but it's not really definable, and then, finally, I can't find it at all anymore.

After a while I don't really feel the bed under me either. So now the ceiling is blurred, and I can't really feel what's suspending me. It just sort of feels like I'm floating.

Yeah, that's it. I'm just there floating.

Floating and waiting.

And hoping Jaycee will come back for me.

19

That's what I'm doing, floating in that weird way—or maybe I'm sleeping—when Jaycee bursts back in.

I don't hear the card key slide in the lock or the handle turn, just the door bang open, and there she is, standing in front of me, out of breath, her hood up, her cheeks bright pink from the cold.

"Let's go, Lennie." She kicks my leg. "Come on. There's an Albany bus back at eleven."

I don't mind that she calls me Lennie. I take it as a sign that she doesn't hate me.

"Of course I don't," she says. "Now get your ass in gear."

I force myself up. "What time is it? We'll get home at like four in the morning."

"It's late, but we just missed the last one. The good news is, the next one is express to Albany. No stops, so it gets in at two-thirty. You said you wanted to get home. I'm getting you home. Come on, wuss, let's go." She makes a face. It's intense, but it's definitely not mad. I try, but I just can't get myself moving yet. "Come on, Nick. We gotta pack up, check out, and get there and all."

"Okay, okay." I stand up and start to look around, to gather my things, but I feel all confused and woozy. "I've gotta get my stuff from the bathroom." I brush past her. "Where the heck did you go?" I call.

"Concierge. Then deli. Then drugstore. Basically."

"Basically?"

"Yeah, basically."

"Okay then, concierge, what for?"

"Bus schedule."

"Right." I stare at myself in the bathroom mirror and rub my hands through my hair. I'm a disaster. A total mess. I wonder how long I was sleeping.

I take a washcloth, soap it up, and clean my face. I grab my toothbrush and my toothpaste and wonder for a second if I should brush, but I can't be bothered and walk out.

"Deli?" I ask when she comes into view again.

"Dinner." She unzips her backpack and pulls out a paper bag and waves it proudly in the air. "I figured we'd get hungry. Lunch was a bust, so we haven't really eaten since breakfast."

"Don't remind me," I say, then add, "but you shouldn't have gone wandering around alone without me. In the dark and all, you know." The minute I say it, I'm embarrassed at how stupid it is.

Jaycee rolls her eyes and laughs.

"Yes, without Mr. Daring and Brave to protect me." At least she laughs. "Sorry," she adds, punching my shoulder as I pass. "I didn't mean it."

"Yes you did. But it doesn't matter."

"I didn't, Nick."

"No problem," I say. "And anyway, you're right. It's true. And I'm sorry too, by the way."

"For what?"

"Whatever."

I take one more look around and indicate I'm ready to leave. I hike my backpack over my shoulder and start for the door, but she says, "Shoot. I'd better check the other room." I'm glad she's more with it than I am.

I stand by the door and wait as she runs into the next room and shuffles around in there, banging drawers open and shut and stuff. Then she comes back toward me, laughing again.

"Here. You almost forgot this." She tosses the rectal thermometer at me. "Good catch," she says. I make a face at her. "What? You never know . . ."

She pushes me forward, toward the door and out, keeping her hand on my shoulder as we walk. The door closes behind us. Hotel room, gone. It's weird how sad the sound of it clicking shut makes me feel.

"Hey, Nick," she says when we turn down the hall to the elevators.

"Yeah?"

"You're not a wuss, seriously. You saved my life."

We reach the elevators and I press the down button. The doors to our right open immediately and we step in. I turn around like a normal person, facing out, but of course Jaycee doesn't. She stays facing backward, toward me. Right in front of me. It makes me uncomfortable.

"I didn't save your life," I say. "It was a fever. It wasn't a big deal."

"Yes it was. I was scared. And you took care of me. You fed me ice chips," she says. She looks straight at me, apologetically, with those gorgeous gray-blue eyes. "You're the Fever King for sure."

"Oh great," I say sarcastically.

"It is great. It's really, really great." She leans into me and kisses me. Not like a peck either. Her whole warm mouth on mine, over mine, her tongue moving all around in there. And she just keeps kissing and kissing me.

It's the nicest thing I've ever felt, in my whole entire life.

I wrap my arms around her, and feel her there, and kiss her back completely. My lips on hers, our tongues mixing together. And so Jeremy's right. Because it's not a problem. Somehow, when it happens, you just know what to do.

And as we kiss I float, so yeah, I'm floating again. But this time, in a good way. Like floating and melting and kissing and smiling, all at the very same time. Until the doors open, which happens way too soon. Then she grabs my arm and says, "Yum," and drags me out through the lobby.

The bus station is pretty much deserted. The ticket window is open, but nobody's inside except one old guy sleeping on the benches. Two buses sit idling outside, their dim interior lights on. A few taxis are lined up at the curb. We find the bus that scrolls Albany on the sign above the front window— the other reads Penn Station / NYC / JFK Int'l Airport—and head toward it. The doors are open, but nobody else is on board. Not even the driver. Jaycee nudges me in anyway.

"You think we can?" I ask.

"Why not?" Jaycee says.

We climb the steps, this time her behind me. I reach back and take her hand. It feels a little weird to board a totally empty bus late at night, but Jaycee is her usual undeterred self, cracking jokes about how we'll never manage to find a seat.

She knees my butt to keep moving toward the back, but I'm thinking we shouldn't go that far. "Let's not go all the way back," I say. "No one will know that we're in here."

"And, what? We'll be murdered and they'll never find the bodies?"

I laugh, but it kind of creeps me out. I'm half wishing we'd spent the night at the hotel.

But then as soon as we slide in and toss the backpacks into the empty seat across the aisle, we start kissing again, and I'm not really caring too much where we are. It totally sends me floating in that crazy good way again.

We make out until, suddenly, she pushes me away. "Hold on a sec, I need to get something," she says, leaning across to grab her backpack. I'm wondering if I did anything wrong. Maybe my breath stinks and I need some mints or something. She turns her back on me and searches through her bag, then pulls out something that crinkles.

I watch out the window because it seems like she wants her privacy. Finally she taps me on the shoulder.

"O-kray, reh-gree," she says, sounding all muffled and strange.

I turn back and laugh. She's got a plastic bag in her lap, and a pair of big red wax lips popping off her face. You know, the sweet-smelling candy kind you get on Halloween? Her eyes sparkle happily above them. She pulls me into her again and smushes her wax lips onto my real ones. It's ridiculous, and tasty, so of course I'm laughing hard.

"Hey, where'd you get those?" I say, stopping her.

"Here." She pulls them out of her mouth for second, sucks the drool from the part where you bite. "Drugstore. After the concierge and deli. You forgot to ask about that stop before. They had a pretty decent Halloween supply, so you get to have some too." She tosses a pair at me still wrapped in cellophane. "They're Wack-O-Wax," she says, smiling, "cuz you're a wacko."

I tear them open and stick them in, then look at her for inspection. "That's more like it." She puts hers back in too. "Now you can kith gne."

We mash our wax lips together and fall down in the seat and fool around some more. I feel just about giddy now, so I let my hand wander bravely in under the bottom of her sweatshirt and onto the soft warm skin of her stomach. I'm absolutely amazed that I'm touching a girl, any girl, let alone Jaycee. I let it go a little higher, my heart pounding, to where I can feel the edge of her bra. She squirms under me, but in a way that makes me think everything's good and okay. It feels so nice and electric, so now I'm thinking I might want to try even a little more, when a man's voice booms, "Hey, what's going on in here?"

We bolt upright. A large guy—blue pants, white shirt, blue jacket—stands there, arms folded across his chest. I realize we must look ridiculous, two kids making out with giant wax lips on their faces. Not to mention, I have to shift my position to hide some things, which I'm hoping nobody notices. But the guy just forces a tired smile and says, "I didn't mean to startle you," then lowers his glasses and adds, "Nice lips you got there."

He's trying to be friendly, but his teeth are yellowish and his thin brown hair is brushed over his forehead in greasy strands, which makes him look sort of creepy. Plus his shirt is half-tucked, a pack of cigarettes jutting from the front pocket. Or maybe it's just being alone at this hour, and not his appearance, that gives me the heebie-jeebies. But his jacket has a Trailways logo on it, so at least it's clear he is the driver and not a serial killer. Although nothing says he couldn't be both.

"So, you kids going to Albany, I take it?" He jangles coins in his pocket.

"Yessir." Jaycee salutes him, but at least she's taken her lips out. I pull mine out too and elbow her.

"No parents this late?"

"Nope," she says. "I was visiting my dad with my boyfriend. The folks are divorced, you know." He studies her thoughtfully, then leans against the aisle seat and pulls out a ticket punch.

"You got tickets?"

Jaycee digs for them, hands them over. The girl is truly amazing. I had forgotten all about them, would've had no freaking idea where they were. If it were up to me, we'd be walking back to Glenbrook at this point. He takes them from her, punches them, and puts them in his pocket. "Okay then." He glances at his watch. "Well it's after eleven, so it looks like it's just the three of us."

"Looks that way," Jaycee answers.

"We should make good time. No stops. Figure three hours."

"Aye, aye, Captain." She smiles. "Want some lips for the ride?"

178

He lowers his glasses and eyes her. It's stern, like, "Don't mess with me," but she laughs anyway. He shakes his head, then lumbers up the aisle to his seat and adjusts his mirror so he can see us back where we are. Then he closes the doors, gives a short, soft blow on the horn, and lurches us the heck out of Rochester.

20

As the bus makes its way onto the ramp for the express-way, I stare out the window and try to get a handle on the jumbled mess of things that I feel. I mean, there's kissing Jaycee, which is awesome. I could do it forever, and it makes me totally happy inside. But then there's this part of me that's still upset about Dad, and worried about Mom, and not sure how I feel about Jeremy.

On the one hand, I dread seeing my brother. I can already hear him gloating about how right he was about Dad, about how I'm so freaking naïve. On the other hand, he's seemed different the last few days, genuinely worried and checking in on me, like maybe he actually gives a crap how I am. There must be six or seven texts from him already, just since this afternoon. So part of me misses him and wants to talk to him about everything too.

It's weird how it feels like so much has changed even

though I've only been gone a short time. I mean, tomorrow is Sunday. Mom won't even be back from Philly. Yet there's this part of me that feels like I've been gone forever, and I just really want to get home.

But then there's this other part of me that feels sad to be leaving Rochester because it felt like this cool, suspended place where the old Nick morphed into a new Nick who's a little more bold and self-assured. Honestly, I'm afraid he'll disappear the minute I set foot back home.

So I'm just sitting there thinking all this, trying to sort it out in my head, when Jaycee starts kissing me all over again. Which is nice, because I guess she's not sick of it either. So we hang out and kiss some more, letting everything else fall away. This time, my fingers even brave the soft, cottony swells of her bra. Finally my stomach lets out a loud embarrassing growl. I mean, it must be close to midnight, so it's been like fifteen hours since we've eaten.

"Time out, I've got stuff." Jaycee pushes me off her and wipes her mouth with her sleeve. She gets her backpack again and rifles through. I lean in to see what she's got in there now, but she quickly twists away. I look out the window instead.

Outside, the road is dark and quiet, but for a car passing here or there. We're in the middle of the boonies, God knows where. It occurs to me that we could pull out the GPS, plug in our home address, and find out how far there is to go, but

I guess it doesn't matter. I listen to Jaycee rattle things in her bag and do whatever kooky thing is so very private in there. Then there's the sound of the zipper again, and the crinkle of the paper bag.

"Okay," she says, and I turn. She's got the deli bag propped in her lap. No wax lips, no other secret surprises. Sometimes you don't try to figure her out.

"Tuna or turkey?" she asks. She holds out two sandwiches wrapped in white deli paper, then drops one in her lap and digs in the bag again. "Or ham with mayo?"

I smile. The girl is always prepared. "Turkey," I say, tapping the one she holds higher.

She rolls her eyes. "Turkey for a turkey, of course."

"Then you'll pick ham," I say.

After that, we eat quietly, because we're both probably running out of steam. I suddenly wish that Jaycee had brought another book along to read. Even some dumb old classic. I lift her backpack from the floor by her feet where she's dropped it and start to unzip it without thinking.

"Hey, give me that!" she snaps, which surprises me, because I figure I've pretty much seen everything important in there. Maybe she does have some secret.

"Sorry." I drop it back down and raise my hands. "Don't shoot. I wasn't gonna steal your Slinkies."

"Never mind." She pulls it up and tosses it on the seat across the aisle.

We eat and drink our sodas, and then, I guess, I fall asleep. Because the next thing I know, things are shaking and banging and then Jaycee is tugging at my sleeve like a crazy person.

It takes me a second to realize I was dreaming, and she's just trying to wake me.

I move my eyes around to get them to focus, but I'm groggy and confused. I remember we're on the bus, but we're not moving for some reason and it's quiet and completely dark. I squeeze my eyes shut, then open them again, but I still feel cockeyed and weird.

"Nick! Come on!" She shakes me some more.

"What's going on?" I say.

"I don't know. I just woke up too. Seriously, something's wrong. I don't know where we are."

All around us is pitch black—no street lights, no cars. I force myself to sit upright, then cup my hands to the window. I can't make out anything but silhouettes of trees. I pull myself up and look to the front of the bus. The moon shines in up there. There's no driver. And the bus is definitely tilted to the side.

I squeeze past Jaycee and start to make my way up the aisle, pulling my cell phone from my pocket to use the light. When I open it, it buzzes with messages and makes me jump. Every little noise is magnified in the quiet. I continue toward the driver's seat, waiting for my eyes to adjust.

Up here, the moonlight comes in through the windshield

and illuminates things better. The driver's jacket is gone, but his keys are still in the ignition. I lean across the seat to his side window and peer out again, hoping to catch a glimpse of something. Which I do, only it's not what I am expecting. There's a large tree trunk pressed right against the window. Beyond that, an embankment, which the tree seems to have stopped us from going over. And then it hits me—the bus is on the wrong side of the road, facing the wrong direction. Luckily, there doesn't seem to be a car in sight, and it seems like we're pretty much up on the shoulder.

"Nick?"

I jump. Jaycee is right behind me. "Jesus, Jaycee, don't do that!" I whisper.

"Sorry." She leans against me and shivers, and it occurs to me that she's scared. I wrap my arms around her while I think. "What happened?" she asks.

"Gangs of gang agley, that's what." I squint out the window again. She laughs, but it's the nervous kind. I press my nose against the pane thinking I can see a small beam of light moving way down in the distance. My heart pounds in my ears. It's all I can hear in the quiet. I wonder if Jaycee can hear it too. I don't want to make her any more scared than she is.

"I think we crashed," I say finally. "There's a light down there. I'm guessing it's him."

"What kind of light? And what do you mean we *crashed*? If

we crashed, why would he be down there?" She presses up behind me and peeks out over my shoulder.

"I don't know, Jaycee. *You're* the mind reader, remember?"

"That's true," she says. "Okay, disposing of the body then. That's what he's doing down there." She makes that nervous laugh again.

"Great. Thanks, that's very helpful."

"You're welcome." She digs her chin into my shoulder. "Seriously, Nick. Do you think we should go and see?"

"Yeah, I guess so."

My eyes still not completely adjusted, I take her hand and start carefully down the deep steps, and smack straight into the closed double doors. She stifles a laugh. "Well, why did he close them?" I say. I push on them, but they don't move. "Hey, how do we open these things?"

"You got me." She backs up the steps and moves her hand around the dashboard. "Wait, got it, I think." There's a soft grinding noise, the suction breaks, and the doors fold open. Cool air rushes in.

Something about the doors being open freaks me out. She must feel the same thing because she asks, "What if there really is something wrong, Nick? What if he is a serial killer?"

"I doubt it," I say, but my heart beats so hard it hurts, and Jaycee's totally not helping.

"But why would he leave the bus with us on it? Not even make sure we're okay? I knew he looked creepy."

"I don't know, but I guess we'll go and find out. Or I'll go if you want. You can stay in here."

"No way," she says, grabbing my arm, "I'm going with you."

Once outside, the moonlight offers some visibility. I walk with Jaycee clinging to me, around to the front of the bus. The whole bus is inclined toward the embankment, its driver-side front wheels completely up on the shoulder. The tree has definitely stopped us from going down the hill.

"Jeez!" Jaycee whispers.

"Shhh." I turn and put my hand over her mouth. "Listen."

The sound of crunching leaves comes from down the embankment, plus the flicker of light again, between the trees. *Man, what is he doing down there?*

Jaycee calls out. "Hey, is that you, bus driver man?"

I spin around at her. "Are you crazy?"

"Do you have a better idea?"

I don't, so we wait, but there's no answer.

I take a step closer and try calling myself. "Hey, you okay down there, mister?" Again, no answer. *What the heck?* I look up at Jaycee. "Maybe you should go back to the bus."

"Like hide, you mean?"

I nod, then remember my cell and think maybe I should call 911. I pull it out and start to dial. My hands shake so badly it takes two tries. I don't press send yet. I mean, I have no idea how much trouble we could get in, two kids alone in the middle of the night.

186

"Come on," I say, and pull Jaycee back toward the bus, then we hunker down behind it and wait for the light to reach us. After another minute there's still nothing, so one of us needs to look. I hold Jaycee back protectively and step out to see what I can see.

"Jesus Harry Christ!" the bus driver yells. He's standing like two feet in front of me. He literally jumps when he sees me, the beam from his flashlight sweeping up and momentarily blinding my eyes. When he lowers it, I see him quickly tuck his other hand behind him. "Kid, you scared the daylights out of me," he says too loudly, then adds, "Oh, sorry," and pulls an earbud from his ear.

And then I get it. He's got his iPod on. Which explains why he didn't hear us, if not why he was wandering down there in the first place. He knocks the other earbud out. "What are you kids doing out here?"

"*Us?*" I say, my heart still feeling like it might explode. "What are *we* doing? What are you doing? What the heck is going on?"

"Flat," he says. He nods toward the bus. "Well, blowout, really. Two of 'em in the back. We must've run over something. I felt 'em blow, but I couldn't control her. Swerved up onto the shoulder, and lucky this tree here stopped us from going any farther." He aims the beam across the dark to illustrate. "Surprised it didn't wake you kids up."

Jaycee comes up behind me. "So, you're saying, if you hadn't hit the tree, we would have gone down there?" She takes another step forward like she's going to inspect the damage, and the bus driver backs away quickly as if he doesn't want us to see what he's got in his other hand, which makes me suspicious all over again. *I mean, what is he hiding?* Plus, now that I think about it, his whole story sounds fishy, because even if the blowout is true, why would he leave us alone? And trek down the hillside in the dark?

"So what were you doing down there?" I ask accusatorily.

"Taking a leak."

"What's wrong with the bathroom on the bus?"

"It's broken. Clogs easy," he says.

"Then what's in your hand?"

"Flashlight." He holds it up and blinds me again.

"Not *that* hand. The other one!" I say, like I'm Sherlock Holmes or something.

"Oh, sorry." He pauses, then slowly brings his other hand around. I brace myself but all he's got is a knotted plastic bag with some crumpled paper in it. It dangles limply. "Dump *and* leak," he says, looking down. "I didn't think you'd want that much information."

Jaycee busts out laughing.

Back on the bus, the driver tells us to get cozy, that we have a bit of a wait ahead. "I radioed about fifteen minutes ago," he says, "so likely a half hour before they can get a fresh bus to us. Oh, and the cops. There'll have to be a police report, of course." Jaycee rolls her eyes. "Shouldn't be more than an hour, tops," he adds.

I turn to her. "We're gonna get home at like four in the morning."

"It's okay," she says, and leans against me. "We'll sleep at the bus station and take a cab or call your brother in the morning." Then she slips her fingers into mine and I get quiet. I'm not really sure why. I have nothing to say. Or maybe it's all the craziness finally catching up with me.

"Hey, Nick." She nudges me. I sigh and brace myself for a wiseass comment.

"Yeah?"

"You're not just the Fever King, you're the Saver from the Serial Killer."

I look up toward the front, where the driver sleeps, head back, jacket over his face to shield out the moonlight. "He was taking a crap, Jaycee, not exactly a serial killer."

"But we didn't know that, and you protected me. And I love you for it, Nick. It was brave."

"Shut up," I say, smiling. "I'm sleeping."

21

I wake again, this time to the sound of a police radio and red flashing lights pulsing in through the windows. I glance at my cell. It's 2:02 a.m. I stand up and tap Jaycee.

"Yeah, I see," she says.

The interior lights of our bus are on; the driver stands at the front door, talking, presumably to a cop. Across the road from us, pulled off onto the opposite shoulder, is a new, empty Trailways bus, its parking and interior lights all on, lit up like a Christmas tree. There's a driver in the front seat. I can see her poofy blond hair from here. I wonder if our guy is going to get hauled away. After everything we've been through, I kind of like him now.

"Guess we should get our stuff," Jaycee says. She reaches across the aisle for her backpack, slings it over her shoulder, and we head to the front of the bus.

The police officer, a white-haired old guy who looks like

he was woken out of a sound sleep, is down on the lowest step taking information from our driver. He asks us a few questions, but we're not all that helpful, since we didn't really see what happened. We manage to be serious and leave out the stuff about thinking that the driver was a madman. I don't want to make trouble for the guy. At this point, I just want to switch buses and get home.

The cop finishes his report and tells us we all can go. That he'll wait for the tow truck to come to haul the dead bus away. I'm relieved that our driver is coming with us. We head down the steps and across the road, while the cop veers the opposite way toward the embankment.

"Hey, you know," he calls out as we plod across toward the new bus, "it's a good thing that tree was here. It's quite a steep drop. Sure would've put a damper on your plans!"

I hear it the minute he says it. I'm sure Jaycee does too.

"Gang aft gangly!" I call back to him, because I can't help myself anymore.

As we board the new bus the blond driver gives us a huge, sugary greeting, then says, "Charlie, you must be tired. I'll take this leg." Our old driver nods and slips into the seat behind her like a punished elementary school kid. I can't help but feel bad for him.

Then she starts chatting with us, even though we're halfway down the aisle.

"You two children have had quite an adventure!" She

191

adjusts her mirror. Jaycee rolls her eyes at me and pushes me to walk faster.

"Yep," Jaycee calls.

"Of course, I'm not asking what on earth two kids like yourselves are doing on a bus to Albany in the middle of the night to begin with. That's none of my little old business, eh? And I'm sure not one to pry."

"No," Jaycee says sarcastically, just to me, then loudly, "We were killing a dog and buying a ranch to tend bunnies!"

I laugh, because I get the reference, so Steinbeck would be proud.

We fall into our seats and, like that, we're making out again. It feels like hours since we have, and it still feels amazing and awesome. It's more comfortable now, this making out thing. Jaycee's lips are soft and taste completely like peppermint candy. Which suddenly makes me wonder. I stop kissing her and hold out my hand.

"Fork one over," I say.

"What?"

"A mint."

"I don't have any."

"Yes you do. You taste like mint, Jaycee."

"Naturally occurring," she says. I point to my palm again. She slaps it, then holds hers both out to show me they're empty. "I ate toothpaste," she says.

"Really?" I laugh.

"Just a dab," she says.

We make out some more, then she sits back suddenly and closes her eyes, slips her hand in mine, and breathes.

"You okay?" I ask. She nods.

"Tired?"

"Yes and no. I'm thinking," she says.

I look out the far window. The bus veers back onto a highway toward lights and cars and a big green sign that says ALBANY 40 MILES.

We sit quietly for a while, me just staring ahead. Even though I try not to, I find myself thinking about Dad again. I mean, is he really leaving Mom for MaeLynn? Because if he is, it's pathetic. I think about Jeremy too, and how he actually worried for me this weekend. Does he know everything that's gone on? I remember my cell phone and the slew of messages from him. I should ignore them. I'm a master at ignoring things. I glance over at Jaycee. She's still got her eyes closed, but she nods.

I pull out my phone and press on the messages icon. There are at least ten texts from him. I read the first one from hours and hours ago.

"Hey, kid. Talked to Dad. What an ass. Call me."

I click on the next one.

"Nick, it'll be okay. Seriously. Sometimes shit happens for a reason."

I close it and breathe. Then open it again and click on the next one.

"Trust me, whatever happens, everything will be ok. Besides, you have me (haha!)."

I laugh despite myself, and open the next one.

"You do, Nick. You have me. -J."

"Nick?" Jaycee interrupts me.

I flip the phone shut and swallow against the lump in my throat. I don't want to talk to her about it just yet.

"Yeah?"

"You done there?" I nod and slip it back in my pocket. "Good. I have something to show you. Promise you won't be mad."

My heart races. I mean, now what? What could she have for me now?

"Okay, I promise."

She pulls her backpack up from under her feet, unzips it, and rummages around. And then it hits me how she's been so secretive about it. She pulls out a plastic rainbow Slinky and slides it on her wrist.

"Not that," she says, as if I needed her to.

She pauses for a second like she's thinking about something. Then she reaches in again and pulls out a white envelope. I know right away what it is. It's the one MaeLynn waved at us outside the luncheonette. I stare at it, silent.

"You promised you wouldn't get mad."

I swallow. "How'd you get it?"

"MaeLynn. Well, your dad."

"What? When?"

"After the concierge, after the deli. It was the 'basically,' after the drugstore.

"The what?"

"Never mind."

"How?"

"I texted him. You handed me your cell. On the bed, in the hotel."

"No you didn't. You just scrolled through. I watched you."

"Not then. After, when I left the room."

"But . . ."

"I memorized the number," she says.

I stare at the envelope. It's just plain, like a business letter comes in.

"How do you know it's for me?"

She flips it over and puts it on my lap. The front reads *To Nick*.

The air in the bus spins. I feel like I can't breathe.

It's Scooter's handwriting.

22

I look at Jaycee, a million thoughts spinning through my brain.

"I know," she says. "MaeLynn could barely part with it. Your dad says she's been carrying it around with her everywhere since the Scoot died. Just to have his handwriting. But she said it was yours. And she wants you to have it."

I blink back tears and stare at my name. "But, when . . . ?" I can't even get out the words.

"I don't know." She nods at it. "Why don't you open it and find out?"

I slide my finger across the envelope, slip out the sheet of notebook paper, unfold it, and read.

October 12

Dear Nick,

I hope it's not too creepy to get this note from me now. I asked my mom to hold it until she

thought you'd be okay. There are just a few things
I wanted to tell you.

Seeing Scooter's words when I know he's gone is really hard to take. I glance self-consciously at Jaycee to see if she's watching me. But she's not. She's got her head leaned back and her eyes closed again.

"Did you read it already?" I ask. My voice breaks a little. I'm sure she can tell.

"No," she says. "It wasn't addressed to me."

I study her, leaning back, minding her own business like that, and I know she's telling the truth. You don't doubt Jaycee. That's just how she is.

"Do you want to?" I ask.

"You read it first. Then you'll tell me if I should."

I go back to Scooter's letter.

So, I'm guessing by now you guys either found
my dad or you didn't. And just so you know, in the
end, it doesn't really matter to me. I mean, it
would have been cool to find him, but if not, well, I
didn't exactly have a relationship with the man.
That was never the reason I hoped you would go.

My heart races. I look at Jaycee again, but her eyes are still closed. Her lids have tiny bits of glitter on them. I hadn't noticed before.

"You okay?" she asks.

"Yeah," I say. "Sure."

The truth is, I just thought you needed to lighten up, get out of Glenbrook, go on a little adventure. You gotta admit that sometimes this place can be claustrophobic. There's a whole wide world out there. Plus I was getting a little worried about you. With everything you were going through with your mom and dad, and your leg, and then me, and even Jeremy leaving for college in the fall, well, I just know it's a lot for one guy to handle. I didn't want you to go through it alone.

Which is where Jaycee came in. She and I got to be friends, and then, one day this summer, I just sort of told her about my dad. How I had always hoped to find him and how I wanted to give the book back to him. Pretty cool, huh? A signed first edition.

Anyway, you should have seen her, Nick, how she started going on like a lunatic about wanting to find him. She was so excited, so I just went along with it.

Of course, I wasn't really up for a mission anymore, but then it occurred to me, you, dude, you definitely were. All I needed to do was convince you. By telling you it was important to

198

me. Or, better yet, by telling Jaycee. Because I
knew that once I did that, you would help her.
I knew she could count on you. It was clear how
she felt about you, and clearer how you felt about
her. Deny it all you want, but you can see you
were meant for each other. "Go to the center of the
gravity's pull, and find your planet you will." Yoda.
Episode II.

I can't help it, I laugh. It's a lame laugh, but still. I mean,
even in death the kid is endlessly quoting Yoda. Jaycee raises
an eyebrow. I go back to Scooter's words.

And you're going to need each other, Nick,
because the road is bumpy ahead. Things are going
to change because they always do. Don't fear it.
"The fear of loss is the path to the dark side." You
know, Yoda, Episode III.
    Oh, and one more thing. As for the book, _Of
Mice and Men_, if you didn't find my dad, consider
it yours. Honestly. I already cleared it with my
mom.
    So, that's it, then. I'll miss you. Don't doubt it.
You've been a good friend.
    See you on the flip side.

Your friend, always,
The Scoot

I fold the letter and put it back in its envelope and stare at my name on the front. So Scooter pretty much set everything up, and now he left me the book. *Of Mice and Men,* by John Steinbeck. Worth fifteen thousand dollars. I turn and look at Jaycee. Her eyes are still closed; the little flecks of glitter sparkle in the dim light.

"He planned it," I say quietly, trying to figure out how I really feel about all this. "The Scoot, he set us up. He said he wanted us to go to Rochester even if we never found his dad. So we could get out of Glenbrook, and have ourselves an adventure." I laugh when I say it, because, out loud, it sounds so silly.

I try to explain better, leaving out the gushy stuff. "So he told you about his dad, because he knew you'd tell me, and then you would ask me to go. And he knew I would say yes."

She reaches up and scratches her nose. There are three of those fake gemstone rings lined up on her fingers. One pink, one blue, one white.

"Guess he was right," she says.

Something else occurs to me. I perk up and tap her shoulder. She turns and squints at me.

"Well, at least his plan worked out, Jaycee. You know, best laid plans and all? I guess sometimes they don't go all gang aft agley."

She rolls her eyes, but smiles, then closes them again. "I guess not, Lennie."

"Oh, and one more thing, Jaycee." I sink down into my seat and breathe for a second, because I'm not sure I'm ready to actually say it out loud.

She opens one husky-dog eye then closes it again.

"He gave you the book," she says.

I stare at her surprised, waiting, but she slips down next to me and rests her head on my arm.

And, then, there's no more talking. We just sit quietly and think about everything until the bus pulls off the highway and turns at the exit for Albany. A little while more and we'll be home.

But for now, here we are, Jaycee and me, on a bus in the middle of the night, moving forward together.

Always in motion is the future.

Acknowledgments

With love and thanks to the many people who have supported and encouraged me along the way, but especially to my husband, David, and my boys, Sam and Holden, who put up with my constant requests to "Just listen to this for a second" (and double-especially Holden, who is an endlessly willing and supportive audience and has a great editorial mind); my sister, Paige, who raves and gushes but means it; my mother, Ginger, who feeds me with good ideas, and my father, Stu, who beams proudly from the sidelines; a handful of early readers: Jeremy G., Eli L., Annmarie Kearney-Wood, Lori Landau, B.B.C. and Katie, Paul Liepa, Patti O'Sullivan and her students at Ole Miss, and Michelle Humphrey, who believed in me first in this business; all my ABNA friends, who inspire me every day, and especially Jeff Fielder, who read fast and helped me to tie things together so beautifully at the end; my wonderful agent, Jamie Brenner, who took me on for my *other* books as well as this one; Susan Dobinick, who is always unbelievably responsive and helpful, and the art department and marketing and sales people at FSG who worked so hard to make this book pop (you have no idea . . .); and Kate, who read so enthusiastically and got the ball rolling. And last, to my extraordinary editor, Frances Foster, who fought to bring Nick and Jaycee to literary life and made me feel like a real writer once and for all.